Cover by Rebecacovers

Table of Contents

Chapter 1 1
Chapter 2 9
Chapter 3 15
Chapter 4 18
Chapter 5 24
Chapter 6 30
Chapter 7 34
Chapter 8 37
Chapter 9 41
Chapter 10 46
Chapter 11 50
Chapter 12 61
Chapter 13 65
Chapter 14 68
Chapter 15 72
Chapter 16 79
Chapter 17 84
Chapter 18 90
Chapter 19 101
Chapter 20 102
Chapter 21 108
Chapter 22 111
Chapter 23 114
Chapter 24 118
Chapter 25 124
Chapter 26 126
Chapter 27 130
Chapter 28 134
Chapter 29 140

Chapter 30	143
Chapter 31	150
Chapter 32	159
Chapter 33	162
Chapter 34	166
Chapter 35	168
Chapter 36	172
Chapter 37	181
Chapter 38	185
Chapter 39	188
Chapter 40	192
Chapter 41	194

Treading Water

Jane C R Reid

All Rights reserved
This is a complete work of fiction. All names, characters, businesses, places, events, historical events and incidents are either the products of the author's imagination or used in a fictional manner.
No part of this book may be reproduced, or stored in a retrieval system, or transmitted in any form or by any means, electronic, mechanical, photocopying, recording or otherwise, without express written permission of the publisher.
©**Copyright 22/08/23 Jane C R Reid**

For Jaime

"You are not a drop in the ocean, you are an entire ocean in a drop."

Rumi

> "Every saint has a past
> And every sinner has a future."
>
> Oscar Wilde

Chapter 1

Azize grabbed Saul's arm to stop and watch the human statue posing as a mannequin. A small crowd gathered around him as he stood rigidly without blinking. The silver makeup, from his top hat to his shoes, amazed Azize. After a moment, using meticulous choppy movements like a clockwork toy, he raised one hand, the rest of his body remaining motionless, removed his hat, and brought it down in the front of his chest. The crowd reacted with smiles and laughter, some searching their pockets for coins to toss into the hat while others moved away hurriedly. Saul threw a five-pound note in the hat, and they moved on.

Azize loved London's buzz and was fine as long as Saul was with her, but next week while he was working in the city, she would be sightseeing on her own. Having a history of anxiety and panic attacks, crowds and unfamiliar places could trigger her: but having made progress over the past couple of years, she viewed this opportunity as an important step on her rehabilitation path. But, now that she was here, with the constant noise and bustle, she was beginning to doubt herself. She bit her lip, consoling herself that Saul was happy to pay for her to use taxis as she didn't feel ready to face the underground or buses alone. As Operations Manager for Orion Enterprise, an events management company, Saul earned a handsome salary, so money wasn't an issue. The price of success was that he spent a lot of time away, travelling to various cities worldwide. A week's business in London worked out well, as it was Azize's fortieth birthday, so they were able to spend the weekend together beforehand.

Being springtime, it was a busy time of year with tourists everywhere. Saul tagged along, albeit reluctantly, as Azize perused Covent Garden's craft stalls. There were so many arty things to look at, sparking a myriad of questions in Azize's head. Would that wind chime be better than their bamboo one? The Tibetan rug would look great in the hallway, but at that price, it would be hard to convince Saul they needed it. That cute bolero jacket would look gorgeous on their grandson, Noah, but could she justify the shipping costs to Australia, knowing he would soon outgrow it? Saul wasn't the most patient of shoppers, and although he was uncomplaining, Azize could feel him dragging her away from the stalls energetically. Consequently, she ended up not buying anything, but half the joy of shopping for women is browsing, and she would have plenty of time next week for shopping when Saul was at work.

Saul led her away from the bustling square. 'Where are we heading?' she asked.

'Somewhere we can sit down! I'm dying for a pint. A place called Chaucer's.'

'Yes, it's surprising how tiring it is strolling around cities,' Azize replied.

'At this rate, I can see ourselves having a nap this afternoon. Chaucer's is only five minutes away. We use it a lot when we're in London as it's not far from the hotel.'

'Is it the restaurant with the big square we passed earlier?'

'Yep.'

Azize was glad to sit down. It had been a fun morning, yet exhausting after so much walking. To keep it simple, they both ordered pizza and beer. 'I can't wait for tonight,' she said.
'Oh God, yes, the opera. What is it called?'
'Madam Butterfly. I know it isn't your cup of tea, but I appreciate you humouring me. Everyone has to see an opera at least once in a lifetime. The key is reading the story first; so you know what's going on. You never know; you could end up enjoying it.'
Saul smiled, 'Well, at least it's not ballet, but I can't promise I won't fall asleep.' His smile was his most endearing feature, lighting up his entire face. That and charisma made up for his ordinary looks, with mousy hair, grey eyes, and a bit on the short side.
'As long as you don't snore!' Azize laughed. Saul gazed at her across the table, her dark eyes and swarthy skin inherited from her Turkish father. He had a weakness for foreign women. Azize took care of herself and looked pretty good for her age. He found it hard to believe they'd been married for nearly twenty years.
'I can't believe London's costs,' Azize interrupted his thoughts as their pizzas arrived. 'Judging by the number of people here, they must make a fortune, and it's not even peak season.'
'Every city is the same. It's as well Orion give us a healthy per diem allowance.'
'It's nice to visit, but I couldn't live in a city.' They lived in southern England, on the outskirts of Trubury, Azize enjoyed the tranquillity of the countryside, but Saul found it dull.
'I'm used to the hustle and bustle. City-hopping is my job.' He complained a lot about his work for sympathy, but, in reality, he enjoyed the freedom it afforded him. They had a beautiful home, but he could never settle there for long before being bored. In all honesty, and unbeknown to Azize, he didn't need to travel as much

as he did but relished the prospect of another hotel in another city, all expenses paid, and the freedom to do what he wanted. Of a middle-class background, Saul was born and raised in Trubury. Five years ago, his mother died from cancer, followed by his father shortly after from a heart attack. Now, his only surviving relative was Daniel, his brother, two years his senior, but they had never seen eye to eye. Dan, too, was successful, running two retail businesses, but he was on his third marriage with four children from two of them.

The week ahead was big for Orion, as they would be pitting against their main rivals, Britannia Corporation, in pursuance of a major contract that had the potential to raise their profile astronomically. If they succeeded, they would work alongside the Troyman Trust to promote and organise the Global Youth Promise (GYP), an international sporting event for underprivileged youths, the first of its kind with a global marketing campaign.

Azize watched Saul tutting as he took his phone out of his pocket. 'Don't tell me, work again,' she said.

'Yes, yes, always work!' He switched off the phone impatiently, putting it back in his pocket. 'But, nothing that can't wait. I keep telling them not to disturb me at weekends, but it makes no difference.' Nothing was going to spoil Azize's birthday. As it was, they spent precious little time together due to him being away such a lot. The weekend was about giving her an enjoyable time before the onslaught of the week ahead. London was a milestone for her, vital for her confidence. She had come on leaps and bounds and no longer had therapy but needed to be drawn away from her comfort zone. 'What are you planning to do on Monday?' he asked.

'There's an Italian art exhibition at the Tate Modern I fancy looking at.' However apprehensive she felt about travelling around

London alone, she was determined to prove to herself and Saul that she could do it.

'Good, good.'

Azize could tell that Saul was distracted. 'Are you nervous about work?' she asked.

'Orion needs this,' he replied. 'But, so do I, Zia, because rumour has it that Ed wants to put me up for the marketing.'

'I guess it would look good on your CV.'

Saul leaned towards her, his face aglow with excitement. 'Not just that. As Publicity Officer, we are talking major PR: TV, radio, newspapers, the lot.'

Azize looked surprised. 'So you could be famous?'

Saul smiled. 'Not exactly, but it would be another string to my bow. If I were to do a good job, I would expect the company, at the very least, to remunerate me with a substantial bonus.' Azize admired Saul's ambition, but the old adage about being careful about what you wish for came to mind.

'This weekend is important for you, too, Saul,' she said, looking into his eyes adoringly. 'You work so hard; there isn't enough balance in your life. Just try to forget about work, just for the weekend.' Five years older than her, his hair revealed the occasional shot of grey, and the laughter lines around his eyes were quite charming. Even after all these years, despite the ups and downs faced by all marriages, they were still close.

Saul sighed. 'You're right, love. I've got so used to thinking about work, but it's not healthy for the old ticker, is it?' He patted his heart affectionately.

'No, it isn't. Honestly, I'm grateful to you for providing us with such a lovely home and a great lifestyle. However, success has a high price to pay, Saul, and I worry about you. I wish you would take more time off.'

Saul looked at her intently. 'I don't deserve you, you know,' he said. And he meant it. If his wife knew only half of what he had done, she would have kicked him out of the house years ago. There was nothing quite like corporate success to feed the ego, and he met a lot of attractive women along the way, taking advantage of the fact that a man in an expensive suit and an aura projecting success were magnets to ambitious women. Being away from home could be lonely, and casual encounters filled the void. Add to that, that there was something erotic about staying in expensive hotels, dining out at the top restaurants, and smuggling an attractive woman into one's room late at night. They all did it at Orion, both men and women. It was, after all, something that successful people do, but for Saul, it had never been anything other than a pastime. He compartmentalised everything, viewing his life like a house. This room was work; that one was home; this one was holidays; that one was outside interests, and the dark closet tucked away in the corner was sex. Yes, he did it because he got away with it, and: he didn't think Azize would ever get to find out. But God forbid if she ever did.

Saul finished his beer and stood up. 'Nature calls!' he said cheerily, his phone falling out of his pocket as he started moving away, landing on the floor by his chair. Azize picked it up. 'I'll look after it. You won't be needing it in the loo, will you?' she laughed, placing it on the table. Having an uneasy conscience, even though it was password-protected, Saul felt insecure about leaving his phone, but he wouldn't be gone long. Azize watched him skirting his way around the tables through the square heading for the restaurant. She looked around in surprise at how popular it was here as the tables were filling by the moment. From where she sat, it looked busy inside the restaurant too. They were fortunate to have arrived when they did, securing a table outside. And they were lucky with the weather being dry, albeit overcast. Walking around London in the rain would be miserable. Azize checked her phone, replying to a few messages. Phoebe, their only daughter, had tried calling, but she'd catch up with her later back at the hotel.

Ten minutes later, she finished her beer and looked up towards the restaurant to see if she could see Saul. He was certainly taking his time, but maybe with the restaurant being so busy, there was a queue for the loo. This was something women had to do frequently, but one of life's curiosities was that one rarely saw queues for men's toilets.

Fifteen minutes passed. Could Saul have bumped into a work colleague? As he'd pointed out, The Chaucer, being in close proximity to the Majestic Orchid hotel, where they always stayed, was popular for many of them. Twenty minutes later, Azize felt anxious. Damn, she thought, I wish he had his phone with him now, so I could call him. She rubbed her hands together nervously, tapping her feet impatiently on the ground, her eyes searching for a man in a white open-neck short-sleeved shirt and navy chinos. What should she do? If she left the table and headed towards the restaurant, she might miss him in the crowd, and then what? Besides, her body was beginning to signal those dreaded fight or flight messages: nausea, a racing heart, her brow breaking out in a sweat. She looked at her watch again. He had been gone for half an hour. Perhaps something happened to him? What? A heart attack in the toilet? She searched her bag, then remembered leaving her medications back at the hotel, thinking that being with Saul, she wouldn't need them. She always kept them on her, just for emergencies. It was typical that she didn't have them on her now when she needed them.

Chapter 2

A woman came out in front of him as he exited the toilets.

'Christ! What are you doing here?' Saul looked shocked as recognition set in. Carmen! Of all the people in the world, he least expected or wanted to see. He looked at her, tall, slim, dark shiny hair resting loosely around her neck. He had to admit, albeit reluctantly, that she was still delectable. What was the chance of bumping into her here, of all places?

'I'm here for an interview,' she replied. 'You?'

'On business. I thought you returned to Spain.'

'Had you not ignored my calls, you would have known I am still in England.'

Saul took a long breath. 'Carmen, I told you over three years ago it was over between us. And I paid you handsomely, remember?'

'To get rid of me. Yes, Saul, how can I ever forget how you treated me—and your daughter?'

Saul brushed his hand through his hair impatiently and started to move away, but Carmen grabbed his arm and pulled him back. 'You are Marta's father, and I need to speak to you about something important!' she said with a grimace that distorted her features.

'I'll call you next week.'

'No, this can't wait, Saul.'

'Well, it will have to. I have to get back to my wife.' He pulled away from her grasp.

9

'If you go now, I'll come with you. I will come and tell Azize everything,' Carmen threatened.

'I gave you enough money, for God's sake! What do you want now?' Saul said irately, as a customer pushed past him rudely as they were blocking the entrance to the men's toilets.

'Five minutes is all I ask,' she said.

'What? How?' Saul was flustered.

'I am staying at the Gregory Inn next door. I need you to sign something as Marta's father.'

'What exactly?'

'Paperwork for the trust fund you promised for her. I've filled in most of the paperwork; there are just a few bits for you to do.'

'Send it to the office!' he blasted.

'No, Saul. I don't trust you. Come with me now, or I will speak to your wife.'

A scandal prompted Carmen to leave Spain at age 19 after being caught in bed with Mateo, her best friend's fiancé. Living in a tight-knit community where everyone's business was public knowledge, she asked Helen, a pen pal in England, if she could stay with her. They had been corresponding for years but had never met. To begin with everything worked out well. Helen lived in a two-bedroom flat and welcomed Carmen to stay with her for a few weeks. Carmen quickly found a boyfriend, Dave, who encouraged her to stay in England. She got a job as a waitress at Flamingos, a popular restaurant, and paid Helen rent. When, after six months, the relationship with Dave fizzled out, Carmen began hunting for another man, who turned out to be Saul. He, five years older than Carmen, was back from university on summer sabbatical. On that fateful night, he was having dinner with his girlfriend, Louise, but found himself distracted by their flirtatious waitress, Carmen.

Louise picked up on it, causing an argument. Of course, Saul denied flirting with her but noticed Carmen had written her phone number at the bottom of the bill, alongside the letter 'C' for Carmen. The rest is history.

The chemistry was strong, but Saul viewed the relationship more to do about lust than affection. Jealous and possessive, Carmen believed she had the God-given right to own him. This and her volatile nature and commitment demands turned him off, so when she moved away to embark on an Interior Design course at college, his wings no longer clipped, Saul felt free to play the field. He hit it off with Azize immediately. After Carmen, she was a breath of fresh air, carefree and not demanding. Saul's friends noticed a change in him as he relinquished his bad-boy image. He chose to spend more time with Azize than with the lads, and their love quickly blossomed. Saul proposed to her, and Azize fell pregnant. When they married, it should have been the end of Carmen, but sadly it wasn't, and Saul was a fool to the highest degree. All these thoughts ran through his tortuous mind as he followed Carmen out of the restaurant.

The Gregory Inn was a small boutique hotel. They climbed the stairs to the second floor and made their way to the end of the corridor. Saul looked at his watch impatiently. 'This had better not take long!' he said.

'I told you just five minutes. I have an interview later, so I have no intention of keeping you here,' she lied again. They entered the room with bog-standard magnolia walls, a television on top of a unit with tea-making facilities, a small fridge and a freshly made double bed with her pink satin nightie teasingly placed on the pillow. Saul stood impatiently while Carmen casually walked over to her briefcase and took out a wad of papers. He wondered why she had the trust documents on her. 'How come you brought the paperwork with you?' he asked suspiciously.

'Emma told me you were spending the weekend with your wife. I knew you would stay at the Majestic Orchid because it's the hotel Orion always uses. And, let's face it, you are predictable. You always have lunch at Chaucer's.'

Saul clenched his fists. He didn't need reminding of the steamy encounters spent with Carmen at the Majestic. Damn Emma! he thought. Even though she never spoke about Carmen, he was aware they had stayed in touch, but as his PA, Emma should know better than divulge his comings and goings.

Carmen seemed to enjoy surprising people, like a jack-in-a-box, appearing out of nowhere, just as she had done earlier. A similar thing had happened four years ago when Saul bumped into her in The Cross and Gate pub during a lunch meeting with a colleague. Little did he know she had followed him. Saul saw no threat in meeting for a drink after work. He was glad to see her, to catch up on everything that had happened over the past two decades. It massaged his ego to speak about his career success while Carmen told him she had returned to Spain and married Juan, which turned out to be a disaster, after which she decided to return to England for a fresh start.

A few drinks later, just for old-time's sake, they ended up in bed together: mistake number one. Carmen said she needed to find work, and it just so happened that Orion was looking for an admin assistant to cover Julie's maternity leave. Carmen said she had gained a diploma in administration in Spain and her English was good, so Saul spoke to HR, and the job was hers: mistake number two. And, of course, the affair sparked up again: mistake number three.

Then came Saul's worst nightmare when she announced she was pregnant with his child. He recalled her fury when he offered to pay for an abortion, how she threatened to tell Azize about the affair. Eventually, it cost him a small fortune to pay her to go away and leave him alone. She also insisted that he set up a trust fund for the child, to which he reluctantly agreed, secretly hanging onto the hope that it was a long way off, that with a bit of luck, she would change her mind and have an abortion, or else go back to Spain and forget about him. But here she was, like a flea on a cat three and a half years later, back to cause more mayhem.

'Are you saying you devised all this? Have you been following us? How did you know we were at Chaucer's?' he asked.

'I told you, you're predictable,' Carmen replied.

Saul clenched his fists, looking at his watch impatiently. 'Have you been following me?' he asked.

Carmen looked at him crossly. 'I had to find some way of getting hold of you. You don't reply to my emails or messages. If I come to your office, you won't let me near you. What do you expect me to do?'

'What precisely do you expect *me* to do?' Saul stormed. 'I've given you a fortune. What more do you want?' By now, he was both livid and concerned about Azize waiting for him and how he would explain himself.

'Just this!' Carmen replied, clenching the paperwork in her hands. 'Look, if you stop talking and calm down, we can get this done in two minutes.' She walked over to an open bottle of red wine on the table and poured it into a glass. 'Here! She said. 'Drink this to calm your nerves!'

Saul snatched it from her hand and drank the contents in one fell swoop. 'Two minutes, or I'm going!' he said. Carmen put the papers on the table and began leafing through them.

Chapter 3

As the rising panic was hitting Azize, the din around her suddenly seemed to get louder and felt hostile as people were laughing and joking. Saul had been gone now for thirty-five minutes. Coupled with her anxiety, she was angry because, in all probability, he was being neglectful, chatting to a colleague, and forgetting about her. Who could be so important to be spending all this time with she wondered? Five more minutes passed. 'What if he doesn't come back?' she said out aloud. 'What if he has collapsed in the toilet?' She couldn't just sit here like an idiot. But she needed to calm down, running through the exercises she had learned in therapy.

First, she needed to take long, deep breaths to slow her breathing, despite being aware that her heart was pounding throughout. Next, she needed to shift her attention away from her head and focus on her feet to ground herself. Then, say out loud three things she could see and three things she could hear: 'Door: Food: People: Laughing: Plate clattering: Talking.' Finally, she tapped her wrist while reciting the mantra: 'I am calm. I am peaceful. All is well in my world.' It always felt silly saying things that were not congruent with her feelings, but for some unknown reason, it sometimes helped. But, this wasn't just a case of calming herself down, she thought, because whatever she did, the problem was external and would not resolve itself with breathing and mantras.

Her hands shaking, Azize placed Saul's phone in her handbag, took a deep breath and rose to her feet. Her head spun as she told herself repeatedly, 'I am calm,' as she meandered between the tables, heading in the direction of the restaurant. She was doing fine until a rogue thought suggested she might faint. And, hey presto, she lost her balance, quickly grasping onto a table. A woman there in mid-conversation looked up at her in surprise, touching her arm and asking if she was okay. Azize took a deep breath and laughed. Another trick Annie, her therapist, had told her was that laughter relaxes the body and, therefore, the mind. 'I'm so sorry. I just lost my balance,' she replied, straightening her shoulders and fixing her eyes on her target, the restaurant, where she hoped to find Saul in deep conversation with someone.

She made it to the Gent's toilet, looking around frantically, but there was no sign of Saul. She tugged at a young man's arm as he headed for the Gents. 'Please,' she said. 'Can you see if my husband is in there?' The young man laughed, seeming to think it was a joke. 'He has brown hair and is wearing a white linen shirt and navy trousers.'

The man looked confused. 'Okay,' he said.

'Please! His name is Saul, just in case he's um: in a cubicle.' But, when he came out moments later, he shook his head. 'Sorry, I called out the name, but no one answered,' he said, still appearing nonplussed about the situation.

'Oh!' exclaimed Azize. 'Well, thanks.' Then, she turned her attention to the waitress rushing towards a table with a tray of drinks. Azize asked her if she had seen a man of Saul's description, then felt stupid when the waitress replied sarcastically: 'Sorry, Ma'am, but this is a big place.'

'Yes, of course!' She stood there looking all around, but there was no sign of him. Now what? she thought. Had she been wrong to leave the table? If Saul were to go there now, he would find she wasn't there. She looked over, and there were now no free tables around where they had sat. Loud laughter erupted from a small gathering of youngsters, jarring her nerves even more, spiralling her into a world of echoes. She covered her ears with her hands, desperately trying to collect her thoughts.

Chapter 4

Saul opened his eyes, and everything appeared blurry. He looked up, wondering where he was. 'What the heck?' he exclaimed, then he spotted Carmen's long bare legs, as she sat opposite wearing nothing but a fluffy white towel that barely covered her.
Saul sprang to his feet unsteadily, still feeling drowsy. 'What happened?'
Carmen perched herself at the end of the bed, theatrically releasing her hair from the turban, smiling at him seductively. 'You fainted,' she said directly. Saul looked confused, searching the room for clues, his eyes fixing on an empty wine glass. The memories came flooding in, bumping into Carmen and coming to her hotel to sign some paperwork. Then he seemed to have blanked out. He thought of Azize, sitting at the table waiting for him.
He didn't believe Carmen. 'You conniving bitch, you tricked me!' he stormed. 'You spiked my wine, didn't you?' He walked towards her unsteadily, his fists clenched, his face flushed with anger.
'Calm down, Saul!' Carmen stood up, placing her hands on her hips defiantly. 'I was looking for the paperwork when you passed out. It must have been the heat.'
Saul stood in front of her. He had never struck a woman and never would, but in his moment of madness, he had to enforce strong willpower to resist lashing out.

'If you had let me talk to you in the first place, none of this would have happened,' she said, throwing up her hands.

'What is it you want from me, Carmen? I gave you money from my own family's funds. For Christ's sake, this is ridiculous!'

Carmen threw her turban at him. 'I don't want your money. It's you! I want you! You owe it to me. You have ruined my life. If it weren't for you, I would be successful. I would be—'

'Bullshit! Why would I want *you*?' Saul spat.

'You bastard!' screamed Carmen. 'You used me. You claim to love your wife, but you sleep around. You have no idea what love is!'

'Oh, and you do, I suppose. Er, shall I guess, coercion, blackmail? Did you think I would leave my lovely wife for the likes of you?' His words were harsh, and Saul felt like going further but held back. He was angry, frustrated and concerned about Azize, who was fragile. She hadn't had a panic attack for some time, but his disappearance would undoubtedly trigger her.

'You use women! You play on their emotions. You think they are toys to cast away once you have done with them. But, you met your match with me!' she threatened.

Saul laughed cynically. 'Oh yes, and what will you do this time?'

'You think this is funny, do you?' Carmen narrowed her eyes menacingly. 'I can destroy you,' she taunted.

'Oh, really?' Saul made for the door.

'I can get you sacked and destroy your family in one flush!'

Saul turned on his step. 'I'd like to see you try!' he said, pointing his finger at her.

'I will tell Bill you slept with his wife and divulge the derogatory comments you said about them both. And I can tell your wife everything. I don't think she is the forgiving type. You, Saul, will be left with nothing by the time I have finished.' Bill, known amongst his colleagues as Boring Bill, was the finance director. Saul slept with his wife, Monica, only once but had foolishly told Carmen.

'You can't prove anything!'

'Didn't you say Monica has a large birthmark on her thigh? Only a lover would know about that.'

Saul turned suddenly and stormed towards her, forcing her to step backwards. But he was the one backed into a corner, and he had no choice but to climb down. 'Right!' he said firmly. 'You will never have *me*, so what else do you want? Name your damn price, and let me get the hell out of here!'

'I want you to meet up to your responsibilities. You have a daughter.'

'Right! Get me that wretched paperwork, and I'll sign it!'

Carmen sighed and bit her lip. Who was this man who had such a goddamn hold on her? He wasn't especially attractive. What was it about him that no matter who she was with, her thoughts were always on Saul? She had convinced herself they were soulmates, but the time was wrong, and he would return to her one day; all she had to do was bide her time. She had a favourable divorce settlement from Juan, and being a military man, she was entitled to half of his pension. As soon as the divorce papers came through, at thirty-eight years old, she knew the time was ripe to return to England. She hoped that, after all these years, Saul would no longer be with Azize. She hoped he would be available: it would be *their* time. It took a bit of planning to ensure she casually bumped into him at the Cross and Gate pub. After making love in her dingy hotel room, he told her they should leave it there, that it had been just for old-time's sake. But she knew he wouldn't be able to resist her, especially after she got a foot in the door working with him at Orion. It was Paris when things fired up again. They tried to hide it from their colleagues, eating breakfast at separate tables and guarding their cherished secret like two naughty children. But it was only a matter of time before things started to go south. The rows started. Carmen wanted him to leave Azize, and he refused. Indeed, Saul had always made it clear he would never leave his wife, but Carmen told him he couldn't have his cake and eat it. It was Azize or her. Out of frustration and spite, Carmen started sleeping behind Saul's back with Alan, who she met at the pub one night. He was married but very unhappy.

Carmen stared at Saul. If he thought he could pay her off after ruining her life, he had another think coming. 'I was in a rush and left one of the pages behind,' she said. Having separated the page that applied to Saul from the rest, she genuinely forgot to bring it and wanted to kick herself. She had taken lengths today, planning everything meticulously, waiting in disguise in the foyer of the Majestic until Saul and Azize surfaced. Then, she followed them around all morning and found herself in a prime position at Chaucer's, from which to watch them. Then, she made her move. But she had kidded herself that Saul would be glad to see her and that he would agree to arranging a meeting where they could discuss everything. But when she saw how angry he was, she had to resort to plan B to get him to the hotel to sign the paperwork. Spiking his drink backfired; even her nakedness under her towel failed to mesmerise. All had been a complete disappointment, and she would need to come up with a plan C.

'What?' He raged. 'After all this, you tell me you don't even have the bloody papers? Well, I've had enough of this!'

'No, Saul, don't run away! We haven't finished yet.'

She needed to change her tack, tone and body language. 'Look, I'm sorry for misleading you, but I had to get your attention somehow.

Why can't we sit down and discuss everything? You have to get back to your wife, but we could arrange to meet sometime. We don't have to be enemies. We can reach some sort of an agreement.'
Saul glared at her. 'Are you kidding me? My wife is frantically worrying about my whereabouts, and you're suggesting a little tete-a-tete?'
Carmen resorted to her final trick, bringing on the tears. 'But, there was a time when you cared for me,' she sobbed. 'We were so good together. You said I was the best lover you ever had. Please, Saul, I miss you so much. I am so lonely without you.'
'That was aeons ago, for Christ's sake!' Saul was not fooled by her tears, not anymore. He felt like the walls were closing in and was desperate to escape. The effects of the spiked drink were wearing off, leaving him with a dull headache. He hesitated. There was no knowing what Carmen might do next. She threatened to jeopardise everything he held dear to him. Defeated, he sat down sighing with his head in his hands.
'Just tell me what you want, Carmen,' he said quietly. 'Name your price.'
'*You*! I want *you*!' Carmen cried. By now, she had worked herself into a genuine emotional state.
Saul threw up his hands. 'Well, I'm afraid I'm not for sale. You can't have me, Carmen. You have to get it into your thick skull and accept it. So, what is your price for silence?' he asked through gritted teeth.
Carmen wiped her eyes, sniffing, and turned her back on him, peering out of the window at the grubby grey building opposite. 'There are nursery expenses, and I want private schooling for her. I want Marta to have a comfortable lifestyle, so I need an annual pension.'

'Fine! Fine! Send the details to Emma, but I want paperwork to back it up, nursery expenses, and whatever.' Saul knew her demands would impact his family, despite being on a decent salary, but he was desperate to resolve this situation and get back to Azize. He would deal with the rest later.
'Another thing,' Carmen said.
'Oh, God!'
'You will see your daughter. You will be a father to her.'
Saul shook his head. 'You know damn well I can't do that!' Then, anger got the better of him. 'Do you know extortion is a criminal offence? I could report it to the police!' he blasted.
Carmen laughed, raising her neck defiantly. 'I don't think you would get far by refusing to see your daughter. If I need to proceed through the courts, I will.'
Saul paused, thinking quickly. He just needed to get out of there. 'Okay, use Emma as an intermediary. I don't want you contacting me.'
Carmen nodded. She may not have succeeded in getting what she wanted, but she would make sure Saul Curtis would pay for all the heartache he had brought her.

Chapter 5

Azize took off her shoes and collapsed on the bed in their hotel room, relieved to be back in a safe place. It was fortuitous that they had had lunch at Chaucer's as it wasn't far from the hotel. She had half expected Saul to be here, angry that she hadn't waited for him to return from the toilets. Perhaps there had been some incident that had delayed him, that she had overreacted and should never have left the table. But he wasn't here. She took his phone out of his handbag. Damn! If only he hadn't dropped it. And why did he insist on password-protecting it so she couldn't access it? She propped herself against the pillows and forced herself to take deep breaths. She still felt light-headed, and her hands were clammy and shaking. She reached for her pills and bottle of water on the bedside table, making a mental note never to leave them behind again.

As much as Azize liked to think her agoraphobia was a thing of the past, triggers were always possible when she was out of her comfort zone. She was fine going about daily business, travelling into town, and working as a dental receptionist three days a week. No one knew the real reason for her anxiety attacks. They all believed it was due to her abandonment issues during childhood, which, while significant in and of themselves, the truth ran deeper. Her secret was hers alone to keep under lock and key. She hadn't told her therapists or even Saul. She didn't attend church these days as she found her faith waning, but even if she did, she would be too ashamed to confess to a priest.

Finding the air oppressive, she opened the window. Fortunately their room backed onto a side road and wasn't too noisy. She looked down on the grey street below from a great height as their room was at the top of the building. People were running about daily business, shopping, queuing for buses, and taxis running backwards and forwards. Everything seemed normal in the world, but she felt disassociated, like she was in her own bubble, confused and disorientated. She wondered what to do. She needed to speak to someone, but who? She wished Nana, who had always been calm and wise, was still alive. Azize was raised by her grandparents, neither of whom was still here. Her father, Emin, was Turkish. He had come to England to work in his cousin's restaurant in Manchester, where he met Maria, Azize's mother, who worked in the kitchen. They fell in love and arranged a shot-gun wedding within weeks of meeting, a simple town-hall affair. Emin soon realised that England, with its grey skies and rat-race lifestyle wasn't for him. He charmed Maria with his tales of Turkey, and it didn't take a lot of persuasion to convince her to move there with him. They planned it all. It would be a simple life. They would live with his family, and he would soon find work, perhaps following in his father's footsteps as a taxi driver.

But when Maria discovered she was pregnant, it put a spanner in the works. It wasn't that they didn't want children, but the timing conflicted with their plans, complicating everything. Maria's parents offered to look after the baby after it was born while Emin and Maria established themselves in Turkey, and once settled, they would collect him or her. But it never worked out. Everything changed course when Maria quickly fell pregnant again. The baby took priority over Azize, who was settled with her grandparents, and they dreaded losing her. None of this was discussed, resulting instead in a silent agreement that it would be most beneficial for all concerned for Azize to remain in England with her grandparents.

Every year until fitness became an issue, her grandparents took her to Turkey to visit her parents as they couldn't afford to travel to England. Maria had another child, and communication between Azize and her parents dwindled. Aslan and Bahar were Azize's siblings, who she didn't get to know. When her grandparents died, aside from mutual pleasantries, exchanging birthday greetings and the occasional phone call, she couldn't help but feel like the child left behind, unloved and unwanted. Fortuitously, Saul came along at the right time to fill the void.

Azize checked the time. They had had a late lunch, so Saul had been gone for about an hour and a half. She rang her friend Lucy and told her what had happened.

'Well, I think you did the right thing. I would have done the same. I'm sure there is a rational explanation, and he'll return soon.'

'Do you think I should call the police?'

'Um, perhaps give it a bit longer?'

'That's what I was thinking. The police have more important things than a neurotic woman to worry about. Thanks for listening.'

'Please keep me posted. And, try not to worry.'

'Yes, of course.'

***

Azize emerged from the bathroom wearing the hotel's logo-printed bathrobe. The rushing water had calmed her nerves to a degree. However, she could not stop her mind from racing, thinking of all the scenarios: he got lost (ridiculous): became ill: had a heart attack: assisted someone with directions: been arrested: London these days is a hostile place. Had he gotten involved in an argument and been beaten up, perhaps taken away in a van like in the movies? Her imagination was running wild, and she needed to be pragmatic and consider her options. Should she go back to the restaurant or wait here? It was unlikely he would be there now. She looked at the clock: 5.45. The opera started at 7.00, so unless Saul returned within the next half an hour, they would never make it, but in any case, that was way down on the priority list. She looked wistfully at the silk dress of emerald green she had been so excited about wearing, laid out on the bed with her underwear and a clutch bag, her heels positioned neatly at the side of the bed. She needed to distract herself by keeping busy, deciding to do her hair and makeup, clinging to the hope that Saul would return soon. She realised by now that attending the opera was wishful thinking, and it was wrong to even think about it when her husband was missing. She started at the sound of her phone ringing. It was Lucy. 'Any news yet?' she asked.

'No. I don't know what to do!'

There was a brief silence at the other end; then Lucy said: 'Okay, take a breath, Zia. It might sound like a daft question, but you haven't had a row or anything, have you?'

'No. We were having a lovely day.' Just then, she heard a sound, jolting in surprise as the door flung open wildly. Lucy was still talking. Azize froze as she watched Saul, sweaty and dishevelled, walk in.

'Are you okay?' Lucy said when Azize didn't answer her.

'He's here!' Azize exclaimed. 'I'll call you back!' She rushed towards her husband, who appeared both exhausted and sheepish. 'What happened?' she cried, flinging her arms around him.

Saul felt comfort in the arms of his wife, but the worst was yet to come. After a moment, he took a step back and looked down at the ground uncomfortably. 'Love, get me a drink, would you?' he said, unbuttoning his shirt and throwing it on the chair. While Azize went to the fridge, Saul composed himself. On his way here, he had reasoned that the only thing to do was to come clean, to get it out in the open and explain everything, rehearsing his lines in his head. But on arriving at the hotel, he changed his mind. He couldn't put Azize through all that, especially on her birthday. She was vulnerable and such a revelation would trigger her big time. Not only that, but his world would fall apart were he to lose her.

He looked at her concerned face as she passed him the bottle of beer. 'Are you alright?' she asked.

'I am now,' he replied.

'But what happened? You went to the toilet and didn't come back. I waited and waited, then went looking for you. I thought it best to come back here. I've been frantic. Thank God you're here!' She threw her arms around him again, and he felt overwhelmed by a mixture of emotions. In her fluffy white bathrobe, Azize stood waiting anxiously. Saul took a breath, gazing into her dark questioning eyes, wondering where to begin. He had another swill of his beer. All he could do was lie. 'A man collapsed in the Gent's,' he said. It was pathetic but the best he could think of. Azize looked confused as Saul went on. 'The paramedics took ages to get there, but I couldn't leave him.'

'Wasn't there anyone else around?'

'Yes, but you know what London is like? No one gives a toss about anyone else.'

Azize looked at the clock. 'But how come it took so long?'

Saul went to the fridge for another bottle. 'It's all a blur, to be honest,' he said casually.

'Couldn't you leave him for a minute to tell me what was happening?'

'I already told you what happened!' Saul replied defensively, then seeing Azize's upset expression, he apologised. 'I'm sorry, Zia, it's been a long day.'

'I came looking for you.'

'Well, I was probably with the ambulance then. Who knows? Suffice it to say it ruined the afternoon, so let's not spoil the evening.' He looked at his watch. 'Shit! We'll never make it to the opera! I don't believe it!'

'It's okay. The main thing is you are here now. How was the man?'

Saul shrugged. 'No idea, but at least he's in the right place.'

'Let's hope so. I was thinking about contacting the police.'

'It's a good job you didn't.' He finished his beer and threw the bottle in the bin. 'Well, it is still your birthday, and I'm taking you somewhere nice for dinner. Perhaps we can change the opera tickets for another night. First for a shower.'

Chapter 6

Carmen was in a foul mood as things had not gone to plan. But she was holding Saul to account, not because he was Marta's father; he wasn't, but because he owed her. He had never questioned paternity, and Alan was out of the picture. If this was the only way she could have Saul in her life, then so be it. It was her secret and hers alone. She detested London and was in no mood for staying. Her childminder Molly had Marta for the weekend, so she might as well make the most of it. She would spend the afternoon at the health club and head back home tomorrow at her leisure.

***

Azize regretted bringing high heels to London. She didn't wear them often but wanted to look nice for the opera, not expecting a lot of walking. The underground station was heaving. Azize clung nervously onto Saul's arm when she could. Descending the steep escalator, she looked around in fascination at the sheer number of people of all descriptions. Of further interest were the posters they passed on either side of the escalators, and, to rub her nose in it, there was one promoting Madam Butterfly. But, judging by the clothes in the picture, it looked like a modern production, which she would have found very disappointing. Half the enjoyment of the opera is the visual effects, the costumes and the colours.

Every seat on the tube was occupied, and as more and more people crammed on, Azize felt panicky, her space invaded by strangers pushing up against her. Saul looked at her. 'Are you okay?' he asked. She nodded but could tell she wasn't. He realised he had screwed up again, that they should have gotten a taxi rather than inflicting this on her. This morning she seemed to have been okay but hadn't yet faced the trauma of the afternoon. 'Only two more stops,' he said, but he made a mental note to return to the hotel by taxi. He, too, was feeling agitated, his head hazy from the spiked drink. He half expected to see Carmen in a wig looking up from behind a newspaper. No matter how hard he tried, he couldn't get over the fact that her sinister antics had ruined the day for them both. And there was the ghastly prospect of her demands which, right now, he could see no way out of. He was in no doubt that she deliberately got pregnant to trap him because she had a fixation on him and couldn't let him go. Having not heard from her for a few years, he had naively thought everything was behind him, but today his past revisited to haunt him for what would seem like an eternity.

Azize felt a sense of relief when they arrived at Piccadilly Circus, her attention shifting from nervousness to excitement as she got caught up in the electric buzz. London was a sharp contrast from the sleepy countryside she was used to, but a fun place to visit on occasion. With all the noise and bustle, short visits were enough for her, whereas Saul took everything in his stride because he was accustomed to city life and seemed to thrive on it.

They chose a corner table in the lavish Indian restaurant, and Azize was relieved to remove her shoes to free her pinched feet. She looked around in awe at the attractive murals on the walls depicting captivating scenes of elephants, dancers and temples, all painted by an artistic hand. Coloured wall lighting, authentic Indian music and aromatic smells enriched the ambience. The Imperial Maharaja's careful attention to detail fed all the senses, and its relaxed atmosphere was sufficient to soothe the most uptight of customers. 'What a wonderful place!' she exclaimed, her spirits lifting at last.

'Yes, it's a favourite of mine. Of all the curry restaurants I've dined at in Europe, this is the best by far.' Saul replied, thinking perhaps he should have taken Azize somewhere where he hadn't brought Carmen. He placed his napkin on his lap and picked up the drinks menu. He was ravenous, but the restaurant was full, so they'd probably be waiting for ages. He looked across at Azize and realised in his frazzled state he'd forgotten to bring her birthday present.

Azize thought Saul seemed distant and preoccupied in his own world. He hadn't even complimented her on her dress, which had cost an arm and a leg, leaving her disappointed. 'How are you feeling?' she asked.

'I'll be better when we get some attention,' he replied irritably, searching the room for a waiter.

'Can you just relax, Saul?' Azize snapped. 'It's my birthday, remember? Please don't ruin the rest of the evening.' Then, as if by magic, the waiter appeared with his pad to take the drinks order. As soon as he left, Saul looked Azize in the eye. 'I'm sorry, Zia. I'm just angry that I ruined your day.'

'I know it's been stressful for you, but for me too. Can we just put it all behind us now, move on and enjoy the evening?' The kick in the balls curiously loosened him up, and like a light switch, he softened his approach. 'You look lovely tonight,' he said.

They never discussed the afternoon's incident again, but Azize felt unsure. Something about his story didn't feel right, especially the long time-lapse. She was also disappointed in herself because as much as she thought her agoraphobia had improved, today proved that she was always just one trigger away from the next episode.

Chapter 7

Carmen threw the keys on the table in the hallway as she returned from the nursery run, her nerves fraught from another stressful journey in heavy traffic. She picked up her phone as Julia, her cleaner, arrived, showing surprise because Carmen usually went straight to work after dropping Marta off. Carmen took the phone into the living room for some privacy. 'Hi, love,' she said, putting on a sorrowful voice. 'I'm sorry I won't be coming in today. I've got a dreadful virus. I'll give it a few days and see how I am.' She wasn't in the mood for work, not after the weekend she'd had. The pay was better than waitressing, but working in an office was incredibly tedious. She had done well out of her divorce settlement, buying herself a detached four-bedroom house tucked away in a cul-de-sac. Saul's pay-off had also been advantageous, and by the time she had finished with him, she would be able to quit work altogether. But it was his heart that she really wanted. One day he would wake up and realise they were meant for each other, but all the time he was with that dull wife of his, he was oblivious. The one mistake Carmen made was that she didn't get Saul's name on Marta's birth certificate. Instead, she had registered her in her name as Marta Sanchez. She never told Alan about her. She had had him dangling on a thread, totally besotted, but as soon as he said he was leaving his wife for her, she dumped him. She could have men falling at her feet, but there was only one man she had ever wanted but couldn't have. Her obsession made her mad, but there seemed to be little she could do about it. The important thing was that she had got Saul to agree to parental visitations, never having contested his parentage. Marta shared a similar hair colour to Saul, but brown was common anyway. She inherited her curls from Alan and her dark eyes from Carmen, but men didn't pay much attention to these things. Parenthood was infinite, and Marta was the tool to bind Carmen and Saul together forever, so he could never escape.

She wondered if he would tell his wife or squirm with angst that Carmen might let the cat out of the bag. She enjoyed her power over them both. However, telling Azize would be a last resort because if she stood any chance of Saul returning to her, she needed him on her side. She hoped Marta would be the key to reuniting them. She hoped Saul would grow fond of her, bonding with her and realising what a fine family they made. Carmen knew from Emma that the Curtis family had a daughter who lived in Australia with her husband and a young son. But at forty-five, Saul wasn't too old to be a father to Marta.

Carmen hadn't seen Azize since they were teenagers, remembering how jealous she had been of her attractiveness and furious about her stealing Saul from her. But surely Saul is bored of her by now. Men think they want stability, but they crave excitement. People like Saul believe they can have their cake and eat it. Azize must know he is and always will be a serial cheat. Years ago, he told Carmen that he had no conscience about it. He said it was natural for men to sleep around, but it didn't have to affect the marriage. He justified it, saying extra-marital sex was the best, and sexually satisfied men made good husbands. But, she replied, his views were old-fashioned and that women were no longer the victims sitting at home wondering where their husbands were, that now they were as bad. Carmen knew she was a hypocrite, on the one hand, disapproving of the misogynistic views held by men like Saul and on the other, she had no scruples about sleeping with married men; in fact, she preferred them.

Chapter 8

Saul shifted uncomfortably in his chair, trying to avert Danielle's sly side glances from the other side of the board table, while Ed, the CEO, announced a thirty-minute lunch break.

Danielle sidled up to Saul as he placed a piece of quiche on his plate. 'Why are you ignoring me?' she asked under her breath. Saul looked around to see if anyone could hear, then moved away to a quiet corner with his plate, Danielle following behind. 'I hear you brought your wife along,' she went on. 'I thought you didn't get on?'

It never ceased to amaze Saul how many women fell for that story. 'Please keep your voice down,' he said impatiently. 'It's her birthday.' After Carmen's threats, other than Azize, he was done with women. Sure, she looked good in her tight skirts, but Danielle wasn't even good in the sack, and the last thing he needed right now was another woman making his life even more complicated than it already was. Why couldn't women be straightforward like men, enjoy the sex and move on? 'Look!' he said. 'I have a lot of stuff going on right now, and I—I'm going to have to take a rain-check on things.'

Danielle stared at him. 'Oh, really?' she said loud enough for others to hear. Saul looked at her disapprovingly.

'Do you think they don't know about us?' she remarked slyly. 'You're more naive than I thought, Saul.'

Saul was angry. 'There is no *us*!' he said crossly, aware of her eyes penetrating the back of his neck as he walked away.

***

Following her anxiety episode, it soon became apparent that Azize didn't have the confidence to travel around London alone, and floating around in a hotel all day seemed absurd. So after work, Saul took her to the train station and saw her off. Once back in her environment, she was secure again, although she felt she'd let Saul and herself down. Saul was supportive yet privately relieved because with such a lot coming up on the work front, he would finish late and prefer to eat at the hotel rather than take Azize, who had been in all day, out to a restaurant. And, there being a lot at stake with the GYP contract, he needed to be focussed without distraction. Tomorrow was the big day when he and his colleagues would be pitching to Troyman Trust to convince them that Orion was the best company for the contract. Britannia was the obvious choice, being the giant in the field, but Orion planned to sell itself as a company providing a more intimate, tailored experience.

As she unpacked her case, Azize felt overcome by a wave of sadness, removing the carefully folded items she hadn't managed to wear. She had been so looking forward to the trip, but the few pleasant memories she held were overshadowed by the events of Saturday afternoon. Neither had the evening worked out as she'd have liked. The meal was a delight, as was the ambience, but Saul was distant and distracted, obviously more concerned about work. He had even forgotten to give her her birthday present.

Out of the suitcase came the green silk dress that cost an arm and a leg, that she had searched high and low for, yet Saul had barely noticed her wearing it. Now, crumpled and requiring dry-cleaning, she wondered if it had been worth the effort. After all, would there be another occasion to wear it?

With her bags unpacked and clothes in the wash, grey clouds had appeared, so instead of sitting in the garden as she'd planned, she took her coffee and chocolate bar into the conservatory and watched the rain pattering against the windows. There was something comforting about being indoors during bad weather, but she was a sun lover, probably to do with being half-Turkish. Inclement weather was restrictive and miserable, and you could never plan anything. She hadn't been to Turkey for four years, and her parents had stopped asking when she was coming. Even the messages backwards and forwards had diminished. They had their own family, and she was not a part of it, so there was no point. Saul was very protective of her and put his foot down after the last time, when she felt depressed on returning home, saying she felt like an outsider who didn't belong. As Saul pointed out, she owed her parents nothing, and if they weren't bothered, neither should she be.

It was a shame Phoebe was so far away in Australia, but Azize believed her daughter's happiness took precedence over her own feelings. She met Finn when he came to Europe back-packing. Six months later, Phoebe travelled to Australia to visit him, and they quickly got engaged. Being so far away from her family and friends, it took her a while to settle in, but she seemed genuinely happy, especially now that they had an adorable son. And she had recently got a part-time job as a receptionist at the hospital where Finn worked as a doctor. Noah, their only grandson was fourteen months old, and they couldn't wait to meet him. Saul had promised they would visit them this winter if he could get the time off work. In the meantime, the ease of communication over the airways in modern times was a godsend. And Phoebe was eager to share the delights of parenthood with them both, sending videos and pictures of Noah on a regular basis.

Chapter 9

Emma, Saul's PA, approached Saul after the briefing, asking for a moment. He looked at his watch. 'Well, I don't have a lot of time. I've got one hundred and one things to prepare for the presentation later.'

'Just five minutes.'

'Okay. I could do with a coffee. Let's go to the lounge.'

Emma was as sharp as a pin, with features to match, short hair, a masculine face and a straight up-down body with no curves. Her no-nonsense attitude made her great at her job. Saul knew Emma well and could tell as soon as they sat down that she was doing her best to bite her tongue. 'What is it, Em?' he asked.

'Look, your private life is none of my business, and I don't want to be involved. It's unprofessional.'

Saul's heart sank when he realised this was about Carmen. It had barely been a couple of days, and she was already contacting Emma about the arrangements.'

'Carmen?' he asked.

'Yes. We are friends—well, sort of. To be honest I think she only stayed in touch with me to keep an eye on you. She says you want me to act as an intermediary.'

Saul looked at Emma's stern face. 'Ah, that, yes. I'm sorry, Em. I meant to mention it, but I've been caught up in all sorts of stuff these past few days. I didn't expect her to be making contact so soon.'

'Being a messenger is not my remit, Saul,' Emma said firmly.

Saul felt stupid. How could be have been so blasé? People contacting him through his PA was the norm, but he hadn't thought things through and should have briefed Emma about this.

'No. You're right, and I apologise. Look, I'm not suggesting you get involved. You are the only person I can trust, and you're a professional—the best! There are things I can't afford to get out. And with the way things are, I—well, I can't allow her to get close to me, which is why I need an intermediary. All I ask is for you to forward the messages back and forth, nothing more, nothing less, no involvement other than that.'

But Emma was still unconvinced. 'I'm not sure, Saul. She's so pushy.'

'What will it take?' Saul asked, thinking sourly that he was getting accustomed to bribing women.

'Since it's another responsibility, I would expect some financial remuneration. As it is, I don't get paid enough for all the extra hours I work.'

'Done!' Saul said. 'I'll get HR to contact you.'

'But, nothing else, just forwarding on messages, right?'

'Absolutely.'

Emma held out her hand to shake on the deal. 'I'll fire the email across to you.'

***

Saul gazed at each panel member to gauge how they had received the presentation. There were six in total; a couple were busy writing notes, one woman smiled faintly at Saul, and a man wearing glasses looked very serious, giving nothing away. It was impossible to tell, but Saul was satisfied that his team had done their best, although he was under no illusion that Britannia were the favourites to win the bid. Jack Brealson, CEO of the Troyman Trust, stood up. He was tall, in his fifties, with thinning salt and pepper hair. 'Well, thank you for your interesting presentation,' he said. 'You will hear from us within a week or so.'

'Thank you,' Saul replied, assuming his charming smile. 'We appreciate your time and for giving us your consideration.' The woman who had smiled at Saul earlier did so again, this time a broader one. After years of experience, Saul was adept at picking up on signals from women. He smiled back, thinking it might give the team an advantage. When they left the room, Saul beamed at Lisa and Mark, his team members. 'I think that was okay, do you?' he asked.

'Yes, I think it ran as well as it could,' said Mark.

'I'm just glad it's over,' Lisa sighed.

'Well, if we don't get it, we can say we did our best. Well done, both of you.' He looked at his watch. 'I'm off to brief Ed and then grab a bite to eat. It'll be good to finish at a reasonable hour for a change. Catch you both in the bar later?'

Lisa and Mark nodded as Saul darted off.

***

Back in his room after dining on sirloin steak, followed by a couple of spirited hours drinking in the bar discussing the pitch, Saul checked his emails, reluctantly opening the one forwarded by Emma. He laughed cynically at Carmen's unrealistic demands. 'You have to be kidding!' he blasted as a merry tune advertising ice cream rang out on the TV, further jarring his nerves, swearing as he grabbed the remote to turn it off. Compromising would have to be met on both sides, and Saul wondered about involving his lawyer but concluded that would cost him even more. He needed to think about everything very carefully. What if he came clean, explaining the child resulted from a drunken one-night stand? It didn't help that Azize knew Carmen was an old flame because, even though it was untrue, she would surmise that Saul still had feelings for her. He knew how Azize detested Carmen after she tried splitting them up when they were engaged. Back then, she told Saul her womanly instincts recognised a dangerous woman, and had been proven right. But Carmen was not Saul's only concern. While growing up, Azize was subjected to religious doctrine by her grandparents, and she believed that adultery was an unforgivable sin. She was fixed in her ways, dogged in a moralistic attitude. Carmen once asked Saul how he would feel if Azize had an affair. He replied that it was different, that she would never do it just for sexual gratification, that she would only ever be unfaithful if she were unhappy in her marriage, so naturally, he would have cause to be angry. Carmen just laughed.

His mind spun round and round in circles. Indulging in affairs with colleagues was his biggest mistake. He should have stuck with the casual liaisons when he was away, people he would never hear from again, but his ego had got the better of him. He thought of Danielle's sarcastic remarks, but she was small fry compared to Carmen. Carmen was perilous because she seemed to believe destiny had brought them together. Indeed, he'd been a fool using his well-versed charm and flattery, saying things he didn't mean, but he never thought she would take it to this level. In his current state of entrapment, he believed that he never wanted to sleep with any woman again. His head started spinning as he poured another glass of wine, finishing the bottle. In his drunken stupor, he thought about Azize, realising how much he missed her. He felt terrible for ruining her birthday; then, it dawned on him that with everything going on at work and in his personal life, he had forgotten to give her her birthday present.

Azize could tell that Saul had been drinking because he was sentimental. 'Look, love, I'm sorry about your birthday. I'll make it up to you. I thought I'd save your birthday present for the weekend.'

'Oh, what's happening then?'

'I thought we'd get away somewhere. We both deserve a break.'

Azize chirped up. 'Great, where?'

'You choose. I'll be travelling back on Friday night, so go ahead and book something for Saturday.'

Azize smiled as she hung up, relieved that the presentation was over and Saul would be back to his old self again.

Chapter 10

Eastbourne was one of Azize's all-time favourite places. Nestled in a corner on the Southeast coast, it was sunny with a blustery wind, the sea breeze carrying a fresh salty aroma that felt revitalising. Arm in arm, Azize and Saul strolled along the pier, past an amusement arcade, Felicity-Fortune's the clairvoyant's booth, and little shops selling all manner of enticing guilty pleasures from stick rocks, popcorn and pink candy floss, hot doughnuts to ice creams. A long line of blue and white striped deckchairs was occupied by people drinking tea, eating ice creams, and idly watching passers-by. Azize loved the sea, gazing out at its dark green hue, so different from the Mediterranean blue where her parents lived in Turkey, yet beautiful in its own right.

As a child, Azize had been to Eastbourne with her grandparents on a number of occasions and had many fond memories: playing bingo, military bands performing at the bandstand, watching the people, mainly old, dancing along to the organist Richie Manners, at the end of the pier. Sometimes, there was singing with the microphone passed around, and Azize recalled erupting in fits of giggles at people who thought they had talent when clearly they didn't. She told Saul how scared she had been when very young, of the wooden slats on the pier, through which the sea below was visible.

But Eastbourne wasn't exactly Saul's cup of tea. He didn't get the attraction of pebble beaches and prim flower beds along the promenade, cheap entertainment, and so many old people. Nevertheless, after all the dramas and challenges at work, he was finding it a welcome distraction. But this wasn't about him. It was an attempt at making up for Azize's ruined birthday and appeasing his conscience.

'This coffee is disgusting,' Saul complained. They were in the cafe at the end of the pier. Azize looked across at him, noticing how tired he looked.

'Are you okay?' she asked.

'Yes, fine, why?'

'You seem quiet.'

'Just tired. It's been an exhausting week.'

'Are you sure there's nothing else?' Azize knew him of old. Something was playing on his mind.

Saul's heart skipped a beat, wondering if Emma or Carmen had said anything—Danielle even. Or was it his paranoia catching up with him? He shook his head.

'Okay, love, but remember a problem shared is a problem halved. Remember our pact when we got married, no secrets?' As she said it, she felt like a fraud because she had her own secret, and it was no small affair; it was something that shamed her to the core. She wondered if there was anyone who was truly honest. Probably not. Saul was an attractive man, and there must be temptations for him. Whilst she had gotten used to him working away a lot, she tried not to think about what he might be getting up to. There had been times when she had had suspicions—little clues, but more intuitive than anything substantive. She had made it clear how strongly she felt about fidelity, and there was never any question of his love for her, so she had to have faith, whether blind or not, that he was trustworthy.

Saul smiled. 'You're right, no secrets,' he was aware of an inner shiver as he spoke. It had taken Carmen's threats to make him see the error of his ways, raking up his guilt to follow him around like a shadowy spectre. He always told himself that lies were deception and secrets merely omissions. He hadn't lied to Azize, just not told her everything. Everyone had secrets, and sometimes it was kinder to keep quiet for the trouble they would cause. But he could no longer fool himself that his secrets were not lies. Arrogance and ego had driven him to behave in ways Azize would find abhorrent. Now he was forced to face the stark truth that the consequences of his actions would very likely destroy his marriage. Over recent days, he had made a pact with himself, promising if by the skin of his teeth, he managed to get with this, he would never again be unfaithful. In the meantime, he intended to do everything in his power to hang onto his marriage.

He reached into his pocket, found the small box and handed it to Azize. 'I'm sorry it's late, and I didn't get around to wrapping it, I'm afraid,' he smiled. When she opened it up, Azize gasped at the small emerald tear-drop pendant surrounded by tiny diamonds. 'It's beautiful!' she exclaimed.

'I didn't bother with a chain because you already have some,' Saul said, enjoying the happy expression on Azize's face, thinking he had got something right for once. But a voice in his head told him he was a jerk undeserving of his beautiful wife.

That night, while waiting for Azize to get herself ready for dinner, Saul checked his phone, discovering another forwarded email courtesy of Emma. *Marta's nursery is having a Teddy Bears picnic next Saturday afternoon. I thought it would be a good opportunity for you to come along and meet her. And, by the way, did you get my last email from Emma? Love Carmen.* Saul frowned at the series of love emojis that followed. He was still unsure how to deal with this burden, but there were more important things going on, and he was determined not to allow it to spoil their weekend. It was something he would have to tackle next week.

Azize came out of the bathroom dressed in a pretty lemon summer dress. 'You look lovely,' said Saul. Carmen was two years younger, worked out at the gym and had a height advantage over Azize, who hadn't managed to lose her mummy tummy and had become a little more rounded over the years, but she was more woman than Carmen would ever be. Saul knew he had taken her for granted, only realising now and hoping it wasn't too late.

Chapter 11

'Sorry, I'm late!' Serena breezed in.
'Oh, it's okay,' replied Lucy. 'Just blame the traffic like you always do. I only arrived just now. Zia was the first here as always.'
Azize watched as Serena propped several bags next to her chair. 'You been shopping?' she smiled.
'Well, Mick's away, so I thought I'd play. You know how it is?' she winked, and the others laughed.
'Well, it's my last day before returning to work,' Azize announced. 'I can't believe where the last week went.' The waitress came to take their order. 'I hope you haven't been waiting?' she apologised. Mann's Farm shop was a converted barn, recently extended to include a craft shop and an adjacent cafe which was proving to be very popular.
'No, we haven't. You've done a great job here by the way,' Lucy replied. They ordered their lattes, and Azize filled Lucy and Serena in on the incident in London. But, they, like Azize, thought the story sounded odd.
'Do you think he's lying?' asked Lucy.
'I like to think not, but I can't think of any other reason why he would disappear for so long,' Azize replied.
'Yes,' said Serena, 'it doesn't sound very plausible.'
'What does he say about it?' Lucy asked.

'He's defensive, refusing to discuss it. He says he doesn't want to be reminded of how he ruined my birthday.'

'Um. It sounds like something is amiss,' said Serena. 'Men like their secrets, you know. I always know when Mick lies. He is extra thoughtful, buying me gifts and that sort of thing.'

'That reminds me. Do you like my new pendant? It's Saul's birthday present.' Azize said, holding it up for them to see.

'That must be worth a bomb!' Lucy said.

'Yes, lovely,' agreed Serena.

After Serena's remark, Azize felt she had to justify the expensive gift. 'Saul and I try not to have secrets from each other,' she said.

Serena laughed. 'Oh, my love, I like how you used the word *try*.'

'Everyone has secrets,' Lucy agreed.

'Yes, and some are best kept that way. I mean, I did some secret shopping while Mick was away. I kept it secret because telling him could spark a row. I mean, what he doesn't know about doesn't harm him,' laughed Serena.

'That's okay with something like shopping,' said Azize, 'but suppose Mick was having an affair, and you found out? I doubt you'd think that was harmless.'

'Um, it's a huge topic,' said Lucy. 'Sometimes, in my opinion, it's kinder to keep stuff to yourself. For instance, if you, Zia, were to dye your hair blonde, you'd look ridiculous, but if you asked me how you looked, I wouldn't want to hurt your feelings, so I might tell a white lie.'

'Yes, there's a fine line between being secretive and lying,' said Serena. 'Like, does my bum look big in this dress? Mick knows that if he actually said yes, I would throttle him,'

'That's more about diplomacy,' Azize replied. 'I'm talking about deeper stuff.'

'Affairs are definitely that,' Lucy chipped in.
'Affairs are deceitful,' said Azize.
'Has Saul ever been unfaithful?' Lucy asked.
'Not to my knowledge, but you never really know, do you?' Trust was a thing that Azize struggled with, and Saul had not always been honest with her. All this talk about secrets made her think of her own, which was deceptive too, although she preferred to think of it as self-preservation. It was something she did her best to bury and forget, but on a summer's day, it would draw her attention as it lurked in her shadow and wrapped itself in her dreams, from which she awoke in a cold sweat.

***

Saul was in the middle of a conference call when Emma knocked and burst in the room rudely. Saul threw her a disapproving look. She knew he was in a meeting but was gesturing for his attention, so it must be important. Saul excused himself for a toilet break and left the room with her. 'What is it?' he asked.
'Carmen!'
Saul slammed his fist on the desk. 'What now?'
'She's been involved in an accident. The hospital called. She wants you to fetch Marta from nursery at three.'
Saul threw his hands in the air. 'What? You're joking, right?' He realised he should show concern for Carmen but was more bothered about her demands than her. 'Is it serious?' he asked.
'They say not, a shoulder injury and whiplash, but I doubt they'll let her out for a few days.'
Saul was flustered. 'But, why me? I can't do it. I have never even met the girl!'

'Because she is your daughter, Saul. You are noted as her next of kin.'

'Ah, now come on! Carmen must have a friend who can help out?'

'That is not for me to say, Saul. I am just the messenger, remember? I told you I'm not getting involved.'

'Tell her I can't do it! I have a job to do and a wife at home. It's impossible!'

'Saul, you can't ignore your responsibilities. Marta is your daughter. I mean, this is an emergency, Saul.'

Saul ran his hand through his hair, exasperated. 'Why are you on her side? You know how conniving she is.'

'Because it's too easy for men to screw women and then forget about it, walk away. I mean, do you ever stop to think about the consequences of your actions? It's always the women who are left to pick up the pieces, dealing with the dilemmas, heartaches of abortions, the pains of childbirth.'

'Don't give me that one, Em. Women must bear some responsibility for wrecking men's lives when contraception is readily available.'

Emma shook her head. 'Look, we will have to agree to disagree on that one. I told you I don't want to take sides. It's up to you, but I am not fighting your corner. If you don't want to do it, you'll have to get yourself off to the hospital and tell Carmen yourself.' She folded her arms across her chest in defiance.

Saul was flushed. 'Alright, alright, but I can't do it for long. How will I explain it to—?'

Emma shook her head, biting her lip. 'Okay, so this is what we'll do. You collect Marta and take her home. I'll tell Carmen you'll do it on this occasion, but she'll have to make other contingencies afterwards.'

'Yes, do that. Look, Em, I'm sorry about this. It's a damn awful situation. But, I want you to know that I appreciate you, both as a worker and with all of this.' As one of the few people he could trust, Saul feared losing Emma. She knew all about his shenanigans, and while others would gossip, she kept everything to herself.

Emma raised her eyes with a wry smile. 'Life has taught me that flattery is a futile tool men use.' She handed Saul a piece of paper with the information he needed and left the room. Saul watched after her. A string of disastrous relationships had left her with a bucket full of cynicism and a hard-edged persona, but beneath it all, she had a heart of gold.

***

Saul stood waiting nervously in line, totally out of his depth among the mothers chattering like hens. He wondered what in God's name he was doing at Sunshine Smiles, but as adept as he was at searching for solutions outside the box, Carmen's surprise demand rendered him impotent. Two people were ahead of him in the queue; the one at the front being an older woman who appeared familiar. God. Is that Liz? he wondered. As a former Freemason, Saul knew Liz, wife of his friend Phil, from the Ladies' Nights. With his jet-setting lifestyle, Saul had stepped down from the fraternity last year with some reluctance since he could no longer give it the commitment it deserved. Unfortunately, however hard he tried to avoid her, as Liz turned, their eyes locked, albeit briefly. Saul looked away as she was about to address him, then sighed with relief when her grandson pulled on her leg, distracting her.

The portly woman handing over the children was called Sam, as indicated by her name emblazoned on her yellow polo shirt. She looked at Saul suspiciously. 'Do you have a letter or something to say you're collecting her?' she asked. Surrounded by a gaggle of women, Saul wanted the ground to open up. A helper stood behind Sam, holding a young girl's hand. Saul wondered if it was Marta. He felt like a fraud because he had no idea even what the child looked like. A second glance revealed the child possessed Carmen's dark eyes, brown, almost black, and he found it unnerving how she stared at him just like her mother.

'No,' Saul replied, agitated. The last thing he needed right now was a Spanish Inquisition. As it was, he had had to ask a colleague to represent him at an important meeting; all so that he could collect a child he had never met. 'As I told you,' he said impatiently, 'Carmen was involved in a car accident: and that is why I am here.'

'Do you know Molly?' Sam asked.

'Molly? Molly, who?' Saul was confused.

'Marta's childminder.' The helper behind came forward to explain that Molly was away on holiday and that Carmen mentioned this morning that *she* would be collecting Marta. Saul looked Sam in the eye. 'Do you believe me now?' he asked.

But Sam was still uncertain. 'I'm sorry to hear about Carmen. But we have a strict policy not to hand children over to anyone without parental consent.'

'But, I'm her father!' His words surprised him, feeling false as he said it. Admitting it felt fundamentally alien to him, but he had to try to convince Sam because no one else was there to collect the kid. He was angry that Carmen had put him in this situation without priming Sunshine Smiles. Knowing her as he did, she likely did it intentionally to humiliate him. He shuffled his feet nervously, wondering what to do and could sense the others behind him were getting impatient. He thought about calling Emma, but she'd made it perfectly clear that she didn't want to get involved. Maybe Carmen had her phone with her. 'Well, why don't you call her then?' he asked crossly.

Sam tried to conceal her agitation that she would be late home again. She turned to her colleague: 'Can you take charge while I make the phone call?' she asked. Ten minutes later, Saul, flustered but relieved that his humiliation was over, led Marta to the car. Emma came to the rescue borrowing a child's booster seat from a colleague. Of course, something so crucial hadn't even occurred to Carmen! Saul wondered what sort of mother would allow a man who her daughter didn't know to take care of her. She knew that, despite his faults, Saul would never do anything to harm a child: but what disturbed him most was Carmen's obsession which seemed to be overriding all common sense.

None of this was Marta's fault, so Saul tried to put her at ease, smiling at her in the wing mirror. 'What do you like to eat?' he asked.

Marta looked down sullenly, saying, 'I want my Mummy.'

'Do you like burgers?'

'Sort of. And I like ice cream.'

'Okay, we'll head to Burger 'n' Bites, where you can have both. How does that sound?' Marta nodded. First, he needed to call Emma. 'I've got her,' he said. Emma raised her eyes to the ceiling, resisting an impulse to ask if he wanted a medal. 'Okay, so you have the address. The front door key is under the back door mat, remember?'

'Yep. Who will relieve me later?'

'Her mother is coming from Spain to help.'

'Thank God! When?'

'Hang on, let me get the details. Okay. The plane lands at 1850 tomorrow, then she'll catch a taxi from the airport, so she should arrive around ten or eleven. You'll need to drop Marta at the nursery at nine, collect her at three, then wait until Mrs Sanchez arrives.'

This was turning into a nightmare. 'Tomorrow? For Christ's sake, I thought this was just a case of picking her up!'

As much as Emma liked Saul, she had little sympathy, viewing this as the karma he deserved. 'Boss, you're just going to have to deal with it,' she said. 'Anyway, I have a call coming in, so I have to go.' She hung up.

Saul was boiling with anger as he sparked up the engine. He looked at Marta in the mirror, who gave him another unnerving Carmen stare. She looked nothing like him, so as far as he was concerned, she could be anyone's kid. He remembered his jubilation when Phoebe was born but felt no affinity for Marta. But he must calm down because this young child was in his care, and none of this was her fault. He drove off, trying to convince himself that Marta was his daughter. 'What flavour ice cream do you like?' he asked.

'Strawberry—No, chocolate! Will Mummy be there?'

'No, Mummy has gone away for a day or so.' Saul was confused, wondering how to explain all this to a three-year-old. 'But that ice cream is waiting for you.'

'Aww, I want my Mummy,' Marta whined, and Saul's efforts at pulling faces in the mirror seemed to have no effect. It had been a long time since he'd been in the company of a young child, forgetting how draining they could be. He was feeling exasperated by the time he drew up at Burger 'n' Bites.

As Marta contentedly tucked into her happy meal, Saul read a message from Emma: *You'll need to do a pack up for her lunch.*

Peanut butter is in the fridge, carton of orange juice, yoghurt and banana. Oh, and Carmen sends her love!
Saul shook his head in disgust. Now, to ring Azize. Lies lies, and more lies, he thought bitterly. 'Sorry, love. I won't be home tonight. Something's come up, and I have to work.'
There was a pause at the other end. 'What do you mean? Why?'
'Crisis management. I have to catch a plane to Paris.'
'When will you be back?'
'Probably late tomorrow night.'
Azize sounded disappointed. 'I bought steak for dinner for a treat.'
'Well, you can still have yours.'
'No, it'll be okay in the fridge for a couple of days.'
'Will you definitely be back tomorrow?'
Marta interrupted, tugging at Saul's arm, asking: 'What do I call you?' Saul put his finger to his lips, signalling her to be quiet, moving away quickly.
'Who's that?' Azize asked.
'Just Lou,' Saul replied quickly, being the first person who came to mind who had a squeaky voice. 'Anyway, where were we? Yes, I'll be back tomorrow.' He watched Marta nervously as she dropped her chips all over the floor. 'Anyway, love, sorry I've got to dash. I'll call you tomorrow. Love you.' He hung up and went to pick up the chips and throw them in the bin. He looked at Marta, wondering what she should call him. There was no way it would ever be Daddy.
'You can call me Saul,' he said.
'Saul?'
'Yes.'
'That's a funny name.'
'Yes, it is.'

***

Azize knew something was amiss and that Saul was hiding something. She thought of the conversation that afternoon shared with Serena and Lucy about secrets and lies. It sounded like there was a child in the background. Azize had no idea who Lou was. But of more consequence was that Saul was travelling to Paris with no overnight bag, which was unlike him. She wished she had asked what was so urgent that it couldn't wait until the morning. Perhaps there was an issue with a high-profile event in Paris? She consoled herself that there was a valid reason and that Saul would have a good explanation. Nevertheless, the situation made her uneasy.

Saul felt satisfied he had gotten away with it but was resentful about telling more lies. He had barely given Carmen a second thought, which was remiss, but his bitterness of her demands seemed to preside over all else. He wasn't surprised about the accident because he knew her as a nervy driver and passenger, apparently to do with an accident she'd had in her past. Women like her shouldn't be on the roads, he thought. It was just as well that Marta hadn't objected to going with him, but Saul still questioned Carmen's judgment of sending her daughter to a stranger. He might be her father, but the child wasn't aware of it. Carmen was never good at keeping friends because of the way she treated them, but there must be someone she could have called on. Saul hadn't bothered replying to her invitation to the Teddy Bears' picnic, so her scheming mind had taken advantage of her accident: using it to force him to meet the child and take on his responsibilities. No doubt in her warped mind, Carmen hoped he would bond with Marta, and it would lead to them playing happy families. But Saul was up to her tricks, and she underestimated him. He wouldn't be participating in her games. As far as he was concerned, he had one daughter only: Phoebe. He remembered cradling her in his arms for the first time, the magical moment moving him to tears. But, when he looked at Marta, all he felt was that she was a cute kid, causing him to question himself. Was he a heartless person for not feeling more, or was his insensitivity a part of his defence mechanism? Prior to the accident, he had made up his mind he wouldn't meet Marta, as such a path would lead to a road that would be impossible to keep hidden. Instead, he intended to prey on Carmen's greed, settling on a substantial cash sum. He had shares he could sell to avoid impacting the family coffers. Lies or no lies, Saul intended to cling to his marriage at all costs.

Chapter 12

'When can I go home?' Carmen asked.

'It won't be yet, love. The doctor wants you to have an MRI, which, providing they're not too busy, will be this afternoon,' the nurse replied.

Carmen tutted. 'How long do *you* think I'll be here?'

'The doctor will decide when he has a diagnosis. As it's a second injury to that shoulder, it could be a bit more complicated and take longer to heal.'

Carmen shook her head in frustration. She hated hospitals. 'The painkillers have worn off. Can I have some more?'

The nurse looked at her fob watch. 'Well, it's a little early. Can you hang on for a bit longer?'

'No, I can't!' Carmen replied rudely. 'Can't you see I'm in pain?'

'I'll go and ask.'

Carmen swore as the nurse walked away. She picked her phone up quickly when she heard it ring, her heart sinking when she saw it was just her mother. She'd heard nothing from Saul. Didn't he care about her? Was he too busy to call? Didn't he want to ask about Marta's routine, her likes and dislikes, what to give her for tea, and when was her bedtime? No, nothing! But that wasn't all; Emma wasn't answering her phone and had refused to give her Saul's phone number. So she was stuck in this tiny room that felt little bigger than a box, having no idea what was happening at home. All she knew was that Saul had collected Marta from Sunshine Smiles: other than that, nothing from anyone, absolutely nothing, and she was furious.

'I told you, I'm fine!' she snapped at her mother, rolling her eyes. 'I should be out in a couple of days if the doctor gets his finger out! Yes, I told you, Saul is looking after her.' She held the phone away from her ear as her mother went off on another tangent about Saul being in charge of her precious granddaughter. 'He is capable, yes. Holy Mother, he is her father! Anyway, I'm in pain, so I'm about to end this conversation now. I'll see you soon.' As she hung up, the nurse brought in a cup containing the painkillers. Carmen took it from her ungraciously, remarking: 'I hope these last longer than the last.'

***

On Mondays, Azize covered the reception at the Crown dental surgery for half a day. The phone never stopped ringing, and after a week off, and with one of the dentist's off sick, she found it exhausting, deciding to wander around town afterwards before getting the bus home. While she was window browsing the books at Matthews Bookshop, a grey cloud loomed overhead, and before she knew it, the rain came hurling down, so she dashed into the Cup and Saucer cafe next door. At the same time, another woman was entering. 'Liz!' Azize said in surprise.
'Oh, hi, I haven't seen you in ages!' Liz replied.
'I see you have the same idea as me,' Azize chuckled.
'Yes, I stupidly left my brolly in the car. Care to join me for a coffee?'
'Why not?'

'Well, isn't it funny seeing you? I haven't seen either of you for ages, but I saw Saul yesterday and you today!'

'You saw Saul?' Azize asked, perplexed.

'Yes. I assume he was performing grandparent duties, like me. Is Phoebe back in the country?'

Azize laughed. 'No, she's still in Australia. You must be mistaken.'

Liz paused, seeming confused. 'Oh! Well, all I can say is Saul must have a double! I could have sworn it was him. It's a good job that I didn't make a fool of myself by talking to him!' They paused the conversation as the waitress came to take their order. 'So, how is your grandson?' Azize asked.

'He's great. Celia wanted to return to work, so I'm looking after Ben three days a week.'

'How lovely for you! I'm excited about meeting Noah. We hope to visit them in the winter.' Just then, she heard a car screeching, her attention drawn to the window, witnessing a driver jamming on the brakes to avoid an old lady who had fallen and was lying in the road. She was on her back in the pouring rain, her stick alongside her. Azize gasped, bringing her hand to her mouth, rising to her feet to go to help. But Liz interrupted. 'There's no point in us doing anything as people are there helping. Poor old dear. I worry about my mother falling as she's unsteady on her feet.'

Azize sat back down, incapable of drawing her eyes away from the scene. A woman was crouching down talking to her, and a man was busy calling for an ambulance. Azize felt her heart beating wildly, and her hands were trembling as a surge of heat rose through her body. Liz was still watching the scene out of the window. 'She looks alright, thank God!' she said as a man helped the woman to sit up, and a woman placed her coat over her head to protect her from the rain. A siren sounded, rattling Azize's nerves even more:

and, in record-breaking time, a blue-lit ambulance appeared out of nowhere. Liz looked across at Azize noticing how pale she looked, with a shocked expression on her clammy face. 'Are you ok?' she asked.

Azize froze, feeling sudden panic, wondering how she would get home. She forced herself to focus on her breath, trying to slow it down, then did her best to make light of it by fanning her face with her napkin as the waitress arrived with the coffees. 'Just a hot flush!' she laughed nervously.

Liz looked at her intently. 'Are you sure that's all it is?'

'Well, actually, I don't feel all that well. I feel faint.'

Liz noticed Azize's hands shaking. 'Do you want me to take you to the doctor or hospital?'

'No, but could you possibly drop me off at home?'

'Yes, of course.'

Chapter 13

Azize, relieved to be back in her comfort zone, waved to Liz as she drove off, then pressed her back against the front door after closing it, taking a deep breath. Liz had declined her invitation to stay for a drink because she had to get back to pick up Ben, but they exchanged telephone numbers so she could check on her later. Since it was blatantly clear that the accident triggered something, she had given Liz a brief explanation of having been involved in an accident as a child.

Azize wasn't one for drinking in the daytime, but she headed straight to the fridge to fetch a beer from the fridge, then changed her mind as she had recently taken her medication. When she saw the woman lying in the road, her memories surfaced through her foggy mind like unleashed demons flashing before her. She had been at the Blue Moon pub with friends on that fateful night, watching a popular band, The Mad Dogs perform. On her eighteenth birthday earlier in the year, to her delight, her grandparents bought her a cute second-hand red Ford Fiesta, a couple of months after which she managed to pass her driving test. Back then, she felt on top of the world with a bright future ahead. But Paul, her boyfriend at the time, was possessive, and they had a row that night after he falsely accused her of eyeing up other men. In a fit of teenage pique, Azize stormed from the pub and took the chance of driving home, even though the plan had been to leave the car there and get a taxi back as they were all drinking.

Meadowfield Lane was pitch black, devoid of any street lighting. Azize took the long winding bend, braking hard to screeching brakes as a woman stepped out from nowhere in front of the car. Then came a penetrating thud that she would never forget. In her state of panic, as a drunken terrified teenager with wild thoughts running through her head, she reversed the car and drove off, looking in horror in her wing mirror at a woman lying motionless on the road, a scene which would thereafter haunt her days and nights. The murder was her secret, kept under lock and key in the abyss of her mind, never to be brought to light. It was the night that changed her life forever, for not only was it something she had to live with, but she felt her life was a lie because no one else knew about it; *or* that she was capable of doing such a thing.

She recalled living in fear waiting for the police to come to her grandparents' home to haul her away. But back then, there were no cameras, and as far as she knew, no witnesses. It seemed she had gotten away with it and tried to bury her memories by pretending that it was a nightmare and hadn't happened. But it was impossible to kill the guilt that she knew to be the cause of her anxiety attacks, which would be forever her penance. She felt like she had some invisible disease known only to her as she kept her secret from everyone, including her therapists. Only *she* knew the root cause of her agoraphobia, and her childhood abandonment issues were used as a scapegoat to mask the dreadful truth.

Tears came into her eyes as she thought about all the happy memories: marrying Saul: giving birth to a lovely daughter: the holidays: and moving to this beautiful home. But bad memories seem to preside over the good ones, she thought sadly. And the choices we make in life mould us into who we are. The truth is she didn't deserve happiness. If only she could turn back the clock, she would have stopped the car and faced the consequences, which might have saved the woman's life. Meadowfield Lane was such a quiet country road that the body may not have been found until the next day. A chill ran down her spine, imagining other cars running over the woman in the darkness, not having seen her there. Azize shied away from the news after the incident, terrified of learning about the consequences of her actions, but the surprising thing was she never heard anything about it. She never again set foot in the driver's seat of a car. Everyone was surprised, most of all her grandparents, knowing how enthusiastic she had been about her Ford Fiesta. She told everyone she had suddenly lost her nerve. Soon after, the panic attacks started, the rest being history.

Chapter 14

Saul paced the room, checking his watch impatiently: 22:30. Surely Mrs Sanchez would be here soon? Being here in Carmen's house was unsettling, and he wanted to escape with every instinct he had. It was well-appointed and modern, extravagantly furnished with every mod-con imaginable. He knew Carmen had gotten a divorce settlement from her ex-husband, but Saul wondered how much of his own money plucked from his family savings had contributed to such a lavish lifestyle. Being here felt like a trap which was what it was, and he was desperate to leave. He should be in his own home with Zia, not in a stranger's house playing a daddy role to a child he had had no say in about entering the world.

'Finally!' Saul leapt up at the sound of the doorbell. A woman, smaller than Carmen with greying hair but possessing similar sharp features to her daughter, walked brusquely past him without any acknowledgement. 'I'm Saul!' he announced laconically. He brought in her cases and closed the door, feeling put out by Mrs Sanchez's disparaging attitude. Like mother, like daughter, he thought.

'I know who you are!' she replied curtly, removing her coat and handing it to him to put somewhere. He held it awkwardly, then found a coat hook in the hallway to place it on.

'You are not the father of my granddaughter. You are merely a sperm donor,' she went on obtusely, swaggering into the kitchen.

'Charming! Though, I have to congratulate you on your exemplary English!' Saul replied.
'Is my granddaughter in bed?'
'Yes.'
She stared at him rudely. 'Well, you can go now!'
'Oh, thank you,' Saul replied, his voice laced with sarcasm. He grabbed his jacket and laptop case and made for the door, saying, 'It was lovely meeting *you* too!'

***

Saul threw his arms around Azize, holding her tight. 'I missed you,' he said, and he meant it.
'Me too,' Azize smiled. 'It's late, but have you eaten?'
'Yeah, I grabbed something earlier.' He went to the kitchen to get a beer, then removed his tie and undid the top buttons of his shirt before collapsing in a chair.
'What happened then?' Azize asked.
'Someone screwed up the date of a big conference,' Saul lied.
'Did you get it sorted out?'
'Yes, it wasn't easy, but we managed to pull it off. You have no idea how relieved I am to be home.' He hated lying, and now he seemed to be doing it all the damn time; one piling onto another. He was still uncertain what to do. Telling Azize everything was probably the right thing, but he would risk losing her for good, and despite his infidelities, he truly loved her. He lived in the hope that her accident had distracted Carmen, and now that her mother was there, who made it clear she hated him, he would be left alone, at least for the time being. Perhaps, after all, the accident had been a blessing in disguise, at least from Saul's point of view.

'What was the conference?' Azize asked, still curious about what had happened.

'Look, Zia, do you mind if we don't discuss it now? You've no idea how stressful it's all been. Let's talk about you, how have you been?'

Azize bit her lip nervously. 'I had a bit of a relapse today,' She hadn't intended to say anything, but the reassurance of Saul's presence relaxed her.

'Oh?'

'I met Liz in town, and we went for a coffee.'

A shadow came over Saul's face. Karma had found him. Even though he had ignored Liz at nursery, he was certain she saw him. And today, he'd deliberately got there early to avoid her.

'Oh, Liz, yes, not seen her or Phil for ages, have we?' he said falsely, hoping beyond hope that Liz hadn't said anything.

'Well, strangely enough, she thought she'd seen you, of all places at her grandson's nursery. She surmised that Phoebe must be back from Australia. I told her it wasn't you.'

After holding his breath, Saul allowed himself to breathe, pretending to show surprise. 'Really? Her eyes must be going. Can you imagine me at a nursery?' he laughed.

'No, but she was adamant that whoever it was was your spitting image. Anyway: while we were chatting, an old lady fell in the road outside, narrowly missing being hit by a car. Seeing it shocked me and set me off again. Poor Liz had to drive me home.'

'Oh God!' Saul showed concern, yet was more relieved about Zia sweeping over the nursery incident.

'Well, she was alright, I think. The emergency services arrived after just a few minutes, which was unprecedented. But I'm afraid it shook me up.'

'That was decent of Liz. Are you okay now?'

'I think so. You know what it's like; there's never any warning of when I might have an attack.'

'Well, at least you're home safe and sound. Make sure you keep your tablets with you.'

'I do now. By the way, Phoebe rang, asking if we're definitely going out to see them this year.'

'Well, we haven't heard about the GYP contract yet, but if we get it, I'm afraid a trip to Australia this year will be unlikely.'

Azize's face dropped. 'But you said—'

'I know, but we have a couple of big contracts this year, and if I'm fronting the GYP, I simply won't have the time to take a month off. I'll do what I can, but I don't want you to be disappointed.'

Azize's spirits plummeted. They had a good life and everything they wanted, but there was a price to pay, with work always coming first.

Chapter 15

Carmen was desperate to get back home. The accident had been her stupid fault, distracted as she was by her phone and pulling out at a roundabout. It turned out that her pride was more damaged than her body. And now, with her right arm in a shoulder sling, she had to rely on other people, which she hated, especially her mother, Catalina. They clashed, being of a similar temperament, and she couldn't stand being around her for long. At least her presence solved the issue with Marta, as according to Emma, Saul resented looking after her for just one day! And where was he? He hadn't even sent her flowers, let alone visited, Carmen thought bitterly. Everything was grating on her nerves, made worse when staff moved her to the main ward despite assurances that she would soon be discharged.

She tutted as her mother fussed around, tidying her side cupboard. Sue, the woman in the bed opposite, found Carmen's wry expression amusing. Mind you, when her husband had visited earlier, he ignored her, spending his entire time on his phone. Carmen certainly wouldn't put up with that. Emma had dropped by but only stayed for ten minutes and refused to discuss anything to do with Saul. Then, Carmen's boss, Julie, came with a cheap bouquet unworthy of a vase, showing false concern for her. And now, her mother was here, interfering and making a nuisance of herself. The one and only person Carmen wanted to see hadn't bothered. She groaned as she shifted into a more comfortable position, Catalina coming to her rescue to prop the pillows up behind her.

'How's Marta?' Carmen asked.

'She's fine. She keeps changing her mind about which teddy bear to take to the picnic on Saturday. They're only allowed one, which she isn't happy about.'

'Well, it shouldn't matter how many they take. Make sure she takes as many as she wants,' Carmen retorted. 'What about Saul? How did he seem when you arrived?'

Catalina tutted and shrugged her shoulders. 'You're still hankering after that loser, aren't you?' she scolded.

'No, but he has to take some responsibility. He is Marta's father. Why should he be let off the hook? Why should I be left to do everything?'

'He's a waste of space, not interested in Marta one little bit from what I can tell.'

'What do you mean?'

'Well, he couldn't wait to get out the door. You'd think he would have said something about his daughter, but nothing.'

Carmen frowned. 'Did he say goodbye to her?'

'No, she was in bed. Don't forget I arrived late. He left the place in a mess,' she lied. 'He is a most careless man, Carmen. You should have nothing more to do with him.'

'That is for me to decide, Mother,' Carmen replied.

'Well, trust me, I know a bad one when I see one. You always pick losers, and it's time you found yourself someone decent.'

'I wouldn't describe him as that,' Carmen hit back. 'Saul is very successful.'

'He might be, but he's a philanderer and belongs in the trash. But, you always seek out married men, so it's no one's fault but your own. What happened to Alan?'

'A bore and a waste of space.' Carmen recalled Alan enthusiastically telling her he'd told his wife about the affair and they were getting divorced, expecting her to be glad about it. He was a good man and would be a good father, but he wasn't what she wanted. There was only one, and that was Saul. Everything would always be about Saul.

Catalina eyed her daughter suspiciously. 'You're obsessed with Saul! I wouldn't be surprised if he isn't Marta's father. She looks nothing like him.'

'Mother, I don't need a lecture. I've been in an accident, for Christ's sake!'

'But, you're not denying it, are you? Is Saul the father?'

'Of course he is! What do you take me for?' Carmen lied, resenting her Mother's keen intuition.

Catalina stood back. 'I'm sorry, love, but your father and I despair about your love life. We want you to settle down with a good man. We've been married for—'

'Madre mía, not that one again! Being married for a long time doesn't mean it's a perfect marriage: you've just got used to putting up with each other.'

Catalina recognised it was time to change the subject. She opened up her bag, producing a bunch of grapes and bananas. 'If I know anything about hospital food, you will need these,' she said.

***

Emma disliked bed-hopping social climbers like Danielle intensely. 'Why are you spreading malicious gossip about Saul?' she asked her pointedly. In her role as HR head, Danielle overrated herself, possessing an arrogance second to none, despite her plain looks and having to wear ultra-high heels to compensate for her shortness. Emma deplored Saul's antics of infidelity and pitied his lovely wife, but having a good work rapport with him, she was fiercely protective of her boss. As far as she could tell, Danielle was a woman scorned after a very brief liaison. Now that Saul had other things on his mind, and there was a lot, she was on a mission to sully his name for ignoring her.

'Why are you defending him?' Danielle spat back. 'Don't tell me he's sleeping with you! I thought he had better standards.'

'Don't be ridiculous! I have integrity, unlike you, who will sleep with any man to advance yourself!'

Ed was in the adjacent office discussing the GYP project with Bill and was alerted by the raised voices, hearing it all. He burst in suddenly. 'What's all this?' he shouted. 'Why are you fighting over Saul Curtis? Don't you have work to do?'

Emma was the first to respond, drawing back her shoulders and raising her head. 'I'm sorry, Ed, it was wrong of us, very unprofessional.'

Ed looked at them both in turn. 'Yes, it was!' he said. 'Go and get on with your work!'

***

Saul was having a bad day. His client failed to turn up for a lunch appointment, Emma was sulking for some reason, and now he'd been summoned to Ed's office. He knew something was up because his boss usually came to his office if he needed to speak to him. On a professional basis, they both tried to be amicable, but it was clear that neither liked the other. As CEO, Ed had to keep the team together, and there were colleagues he didn't like, but this went with the territory. So long as they did a good job, there would be no cause to complain. Ed found Saul conceited, but his work ethic was exemplary. Saul disliked Ed because he enjoyed his power too much, finding him abrasive around the men yet nicey-nicey with the women.

Saul could tell by Ed's demeanour as he entered his office that this wasn't going to be a cosy chat. Ed was busy typing on his keyboard, ignoring Saul's casual greeting. Saul felt like a naughty child summoned to the headmaster's office, searching his mind for what he had done wrong as he sat and waited. When Ed finished what he was doing, he looked up at Saul, saying sternly: 'Saul, you have become a form of entertainment as people gossip and women fight over you. I have no interest in what you do in your private life, but it is not something to bring to the workplace. Not only is it unprofessional, but it creates a toxic atmosphere.'

Saul fidgeted awkwardly in his chair, all too aware of his flushed cheeks. He wondered if Carmen had contacted him, divulging their secrets. 'I—I'm not sure what you're talking about,' he stumbled.

'Come on, Saul, we all know how belligerent Danielle is. What are you doing, messing about with her? I can't ban the staff from sleeping with each other if that's what they want to do, but I put my foot down when it affects morale and work.'

Saul had mixed feelings. He was angry that Danielle had compromised him, but had it been Carmen, it would have been more serious. Danielle was nothing. They had only slept together twice, and he stupidly thought that she, like him, did it just for fun. Carmen told him he was naive with women, and Saul had to accept she was right. Getting swept up along by his impulses and ego, the repercussions of his flings seemed on course to send his sex drive into a nose dive, never to return.

He felt the weight of Ed's disapproving stare. 'I'm sorry,' he said, throwing up his hands. 'Things have been blown out of proportion by the sounds of it; it was nothing.'

'All I care about is my staff behaving in a professional manner and getting on with each other. I certainly don't need to be apprised of your clandestine activities: take this as a warning.'

Saul felt humiliated as he left Ed's office, knowing he would need to tread carefully from now on. It wasn't a good feeling knowing that people were gossiping behind his back, and he felt like going straight to HR to blast Danielle, but after Ed's threat, such an act would be suicidal. To make matters worse, as he was packing up to go home, Emma came in, closing the door behind her. Saul could tell she had something serious to impart, most likely to do with Carmen. 'This better be quick!' he snapped. 'I've had a day from hell, and I'm getting out of here.'

'I'll make it quick, then,' Emma said abruptly. 'I tried defending you today over Danielle, but it backfired. I've had it up to here, Saul, and want nothing more to do with your tawdry affairs. From now on, you can handle everything yourself.'

Saul was too stressed to argue with her. 'Fine!' he said, grabbed his briefcase and sped from his office.

The day's events made Saul poor company, and he took out his frustration on Azize, resulting in a row, with her storming upstairs to watch TV in the bedroom. Saul went to his study and poured himself another Scotch. He paced the room, saying: 'Women!'

repeatedly. In his drunken stupor, he tried to work out what to do about Carmen. There was no point in telling Azize everything because she would never forgive him. But neither did he want to give in to Carmen's demands to see the child. Money was one thing, but that was another. He thought about Marta. He had no hostile feelings towards her; she was, after all, an innocent child, but neither had he felt any affection. Had she resembled him in any way, perhaps he would feel differently. Then it dawned on him. What if Marta wasn't his? What if Carmen had lied to him as a ploy to draw him into her life? She was capable. He thought back to when they were sleeping together. As far as he knew, no one else had been on the scene, but when it came to Carmen, who knew what she was scheming? After all, she had lied about being on the contraceptive pill. He resented paying her yet more money for her silence when she could demand more in the future. Why spend money on the kid's education when his own family needed it? And, what's more, the lies would mount on top of one another, like building a stone wall. Carmen had made it plain that it was him that she really wanted, and if she couldn't have him, she would make him pay. Saul made a decision there and then. He would tell her he wanted a DNA test on the child. It was a gamble because, if positive, he would have to meet his responsibilities. But if, by some miracle, he wasn't Marta's father, he would be free from Carmen's entrapment forever. There was always a chance that she might still tell Zia about the affair, something he would have to deal with, but if nothing else, this strategy would afford him more time.

Chapter 16

Saul rang Azize to inform her of the happy news. 'We got it!' he announced proudly. She found it hard to hear him due to a lot of background noise, sounding like people were drinking.
'Got what?' she asked.
'The GYP contract.'
'That's good,' Azize replied faintly. She knew what it meant to Orion, and to Saul, but it wasn't good news for her as Australia now seemed unlikely.
'Ah, thanks, love. I'll be there in a mo,' Saul said to Sue who handed him his pint. Azize felt like she was missing out on a party, feeling a hint of jealousy, imagining Saul flirting with his colleagues. 'Well, it's good news about the contract,' she said.
'It's the best!' Saul said triumphantly. 'It's going to mean a lot of publicity, interviews etc. I'm afraid I'll be pretty busy for a while.'
'Well, it goes with the territory,' Azize sighed. 'Do you have any idea when you'll be home?'
'No idea. We're having dinner out, then back to Ed's for drinks. I'll be getting a taxi home. Don't wait up.'
He hung up abruptly, leaving Azize to feel alone. He was far too busy enjoying himself to bother speaking to her. Hey ho, she would try to find a film to watch. But, alone with her thoughts, she couldn't settle. She hadn't been the same since the old lady's fall. Witnessing it sparked a return of her nightmares, both asleep and

in the waking world. Flashbacks of her accident haunted her, even struggling to get to and from work today, having to rely on her exercises all over again.

***

Tired of listening to Bill Bostok waffling on about the company's accounts, Saul found his eyes wandering around the room. Danielle was flirting with Dave, glancing across at Saul to see if he was jealous. But he wasn't, even after several drinks. He took pride in himself that he was a changed man. Before, he would have looked at her legs, then fixed her gaze to indicate he was back in, but not now. He had been a fool, jeopardising not just his marriage but also his job. Danielle could flirt with whomever she wanted; Saul was not interested. He found himself nodding at Bill to infer that he was listening and waited for a gap in the conversation to excuse himself when he went to the toilets to ring Zia again. 'I just rang to say I miss you,' he said. Soon after, he found himself in a contemplative mood, in a taxi on the way home, the only place he wanted to be. Affairs weren't worth the bother. Look at the trouble they caused. Azize was a beautiful woman. He had been selfish for believing he could have it all, but he was wrong. He had learned a valuable lesson about consequences, clinging to the hope that it wasn't too late.

***

Carmen groaned in pain as she waited for Catalina to open the front door. Julia was removing her apron and was about to leave. 'It's good to see you,' she said to Carmen. 'How are you feeling?'

'Not bad. I'm glad to be home, though.' A fresh smell of furniture polish filled the air. Carmen was a hard taskmaster and perfectionist with the cleaning, and Julia certainly earned her wages. 'I haven't been able to get your money. Do you mind if I pay you next week?' Carmen asked. It was the end of the month, and Julia needed the money. 'Can I call in tomorrow?' she asked.

Catalina piped up. 'I'll get it after picking Marta up.'

'Great!' beamed Julia. 'I'll call by tonight then?' She knew she had to stand her ground because Carmen had let her down in the past. She did a lot more than necessary and deserved to have her wages on time. Carmen nodded as she entered the living room with Catalina, calling over her shoulder: 'Can you make us a coffee before you go?'

'I'll take care of it,' said Catalina.

Julia was relieved. 'Be back later!' She breezed out the door before Carmen thought of something else to saddle her with.

Carmen was relieved to be home but resentful about being dependent on others. It would be some time before she could drive, and Molly was away for another couple of weeks, so she would have to rely on her mother to do the nursery runs. But how long could she put up with her being here? Perhaps it was an opportunity to get Saul to step up. 'I know you have to get back, so I'll see if I can find someone to help with the nursery runs,' she said. But Catalina saw right through her, shaking her head. 'No! I know what you'll do. You will get the sperm donor to do it. I'm telling you, you need to forget him. If I have a say in it, he will never have anything to do with my granddaughter.'

'But, you don't have a say in it because I am Marta's mother, and Saul is her father, so allow me to decide what is best for her.'

Catalina shook her head. 'You still want him, don't you? He used you for sex. Is that what you want for Marta? Don't you think he would have left his wife by now if he wanted you? As always, you are deluding yourself.'

'You know nothing about him!' Carmen replied crossly, weary of the same old argument. If her mother stayed around too long, she would be a spanner in the works, thwarting all her plans. When she thought about it further, after his recent behaviour, it seemed unlikely that Saul would do it anyway, so when Julia returned that night to collect her money, Carmen asked her if she would do it if she paid her. But Julia declined, saying she already had three jobs and it would be impossible. Catalina took umbrage that Carmen asked her, sparking another tirade in Spanish. Carmen felt backed into a corner, knowing she had no choice but to accept that her mother was here and she would have to bide her time with Saul.

***

Despite her relief to be back in her own bed, Carmen found it hard to sleep, not only from the discomfort in her shoulder but also because Saul was on her mind again. She found it hard to believe how heartless he was for ignoring her after her accident. She hated admitting that her mother was right, but all the sweet nothings, his charm, and his flattery had been a pretence to get his rocks off! Men like him believed it was acceptable to bed a woman, return to their wives, and then go on the prowl for the next conquest, but Saul had chosen the wrong woman to cross. Carmen had given up so much for him, all for a lost cause. She had planned the London ploy meticulously, yet ended up with egg on her face. Even her notion that he would fall in love with Marta seemed to have been a fool's errand. Who could not fall for the girl's sweet charms? Was it naive to expect a father meeting his daughter for the first time to be anything but beguiled? That he wasn't her actual father was immaterial because he had never questioned it.

The other thing bothering her was that she couldn't return to work and wasn't one for sitting around watching daytime television. Carmen was a restless soul who had to keep busy because if she sat for too long, she had to face herself. She decided to call the office in the morning to see if she could do some work from home. While it was impossible to type on her laptop, she could at least make calls. Anything was better than nothing. Her marketing job at Artemis Designs, a clothing company, wasn't exactly fulfilling, but it served a purpose for the time being. Her ambition was to start a freelance business, but she didn't have the capital. She had calculated this in her demands from Saul. He owed her, and it wasn't as though he couldn't afford it. He wouldn't know what she was spending her money on, and, anyway, it was none of his business. Back to him again! Why couldn't she get him out of her head, commanding her thoughts day and night? She had always believed the magnetic attraction was mutual, but either he was deceiving himself, or, as was seeming more likely, she had to face up to the cruel truth that he didn't feel the same way. Hate was close to love, as they say, and if Saul continued to disrespect her, revenge would be her next quest.

Chapter 17

After hanging up, Azize felt tearful, having told Phoebe they wouldn't be able to go to Australia now that Orion had won the GYP project. It came as no surprise that she was disappointed, and as happy as she was with her new life, she missed her family and friends in England. Azize was a little jealous that Finn's parents were on hand to pamper Noah, whom he would grow to love, but sadly, he would barely get to know his other grandparents. Azize thought of her own mother, who had chosen to embark on a new life in Turkey with the man she loved but, in doing so, had forsaken her daughter. Her grandparents had provided her with an excellent upbringing, for which she would be eternally grateful, and she missed them both sorely. Over the years, her resentment had increased towards her parents. She barely knew Bahar and Aslan, her siblings. As far as Azize was concerned, her only family were Saul and Phoebe. We all have choices in life and have to live with the consequences, she mused.

Saul was apologetic that night when they discussed Australia, explaining that they would be better placed to go next year. 'I'm afraid we can't have everything. Success, like everything else, has a price to pay,' he said as he shovelled down his cottage pie like there was no tomorrow. 'Delicious!' he said. 'You're the best cook in England. And trust me, I should know; I eat out enough!'

'Home cooking is always the best. You look tired,' she replied.

'I am! Things are hectic at work, and they aren't going to ease anytime soon. It seems we're not as prepared as we should be at this stage for the project, and the press is already hot on our heels. Troyman Trust is determined to make this big, and I am in the hot seat.'
'Meaning?'
'I'll be doing interviews, radio, television, media announcements, the lot!'
'Well, I'm proud of you, but I hope it won't be too much.'
'It's the break I've been waiting for, love. This is a great opportunity, but I must do a good job. There's a lot at stake.'
'If they didn't have confidence in you, they wouldn't have chosen you to be the frontman.'
'Sure. I'll need some new clothes, and I'm not good at choosing these sorts of things. I'll be relying on you.'
'No problem, let's go shopping on Saturday.'
'I don't have the luxury of time, Zia. It has to be tomorrow.'
'I'm working. Having just returned, I can hardly take time off.'
'Can't you call in sick?'
Azize bit her lip. 'It's difficult. Let me see if Tiffany will swap days with me.' Azize tapped out a message on her phone.
Saul's phone rang just as he finished eating. 'Yes, Em,' he said, moving away from the table.
'I'm fed up with being bombarded with calls and messages from you know who, and I'm not doing it anymore. I'm going to block her. You'll have to sort out your own crap.'
'Oh. Okay, I'll sort it out.' Saul replied awkwardly, hanging up as Azize looked at him quizzically. 'She sounds uptight, what's up?'
'Just work! I'm afraid I'll have to go into the office for an hour or two.'

Azize was disappointed. 'Damn! Well, perhaps we can have lunch in town tomorrow after shopping, as Tiffany just got back, agreeing to cover my shift.' But she noticed a change in Saul's mood. 'Yes, an excellent idea,' he replied absent-mindedly.

***

Saul stood impatiently outside Carmen's front door. It was time to sort everything out once and for all. He had enough on his plate and was at the end of his tether with this loathsome woman. He was tired, and this was the last place he wanted to be, but out of all options, the dastardly deed had to be done.

Carmen's mother opened the door, staring at him with cold dark eyes. 'What do *you* want?' she asked suspiciously.

'I need to speak to Carmen,' Saul replied, hearing Carmen in the background asking who it was.

'Well, she doesn't want to speak with *you*!' Catalina replied.

Saul moved closer, putting one foot on the doorstep, saying, 'I don't think it's for you to decide.'

'It's that rat of a man!' Catalina called out to her daughter in Spanish, her anger spiralling when Carmen told her to let him in. She stifled an impulse to throw the door back in Saul's face as she opened it wider. Saul followed her into the living room, where Carmen was in a chair, her arm in a sling and had a nasty bruise on her cheekbone, but other than that, even in these circumstances, she didn't appear fragile; that was something she would never be. But she was put out that Saul hadn't given her any notice of coming, so she could have made herself more presentable. Catalina stood at the doorway with her arms folded across her chest until Carmen told her in Spanish to leave the room.

Catalina frowned, then walked out reluctantly, muttering under her breath. 'And close the door!' Carmen said. She looked across at Saul, who had found himself a chair by the fireplace. 'You took your time! I thought you would never come!' she said, all the more angry that he hadn't brought her flowers.

Saul leaned forward, fixing his gaze on her. Was she so deluded to believe he was here because he cared about her? Such a prospect was both unnerving and irritating, but his inner voice reminded him to be calm and civil because there was a lot at stake, and she was dangerous. The words from her foul mouth could destroy all that he held dear in a heartbeat. So he selected his words carefully. 'You must be relieved to be back home.'

'Dear God, that hospital was grim! I take it you've been too busy at work to bother about me?'

'Work has been very busy,' he replied.

'The Troyman project?'

Saul wondered how she knew about it, surmising that Emma must have told her. Carmen's agreeable manner was catching Saul off-guard, but he would play the game. 'Yes, we got it!'

'That's great!'

'Yes.' In no mood for chit-chat, Saul shifted uncomfortably.

'Isn't Marta adorable?' she asked.

Saul felt a quiver in his stomach. 'She is, yes.'

'So, how about coming over on Saturday?'

Here we go, thought Saul. 'I can't, not this weekend, nor *any* for that matter. I'm too busy, and I have Zia to consider.'

In a flash, Carmen's demeanour changed chillingly, her glare as deadly as Medusa's. 'Really?' she cried. 'You have wrecked my life, and now you are doing the same to an innocent child, your daughter! My mother is right; you *are* a rat!' Just then, Catalina, who must have been listening from behind the door, burst in, pointing at Saul. 'Go now!' she cried.

Carmen rolled her eyes crossly. 'Mum, leave this to me!' Catalina left, slamming the door behind her. Carmen shook her head, swearing some Spanish words Saul had heard her say before and could only guess the meaning. 'Look!' he said. 'The best I can offer is remuneration.'

Carmen was livid. Saul's presence here tonight had proffered her a final glimmer of hope that seeing his daughter had, after all, brought him to his senses. But she was wrong. He was here to do what he was so good at, trying to crawl out of the ugly hole he had dug for himself.

'Money! You think you can pay me off; that is all it takes?' She flinched as she hurt her shoulder after a sudden movement.

Saul was losing his patience, and it was time to play his final card. 'I don't even know the kid is mine!' he said.

'Kid? Kid? Is that all your daughter is to you, a kid?'

Saul felt a tinge of guilt; after all, the girl was innocent in all of this. 'Sorry. Marta is cute and a great girl, but how do I know I am her father?' He noticed a brief glimpse of uncertainty as Carmen processed his words. Was he right? Had he, quite by accident, managed to trip her up? Could it be that he was not the father after all?

'Of course, she is yours! Are you calling me a whore now? I am not like you!'

'Well, I only have your word for it,' he replied, feeling more confident. 'I want the evidence: and if I am her father, *then* we will consider the terms.' For the first time, he felt he had gained some control. He stood up. 'Make the arrangements for a DNA test. If I am the father, I'll step up, but not before.' He made for the door.

'That's right, just run away! Go back to your beloved wife! You are a rat of the worst kind,' she spat.

Saul turned back and looked at her. 'Oh, and don't bother Emma anymore. She wants no more involvement, okay? You'll have to send any future correspondence to me at work,' he said, opening the door abruptly to surprise Catalina, who he knew was on the other side. She jumped, bringing a wide grin to his face.

'You will be hearing from me, Saul Curtis!' Carmen blasted after him. As he left the house, he heard mother and daughter squabbling in Spanish. Driving home, he considered his options. Until Carmen presented proof of paternity, all she had was her word against his, and Zia already knew what she was like. He smiled, glad that finally he had the upper hand and had bought himself some time, during which he intended to drag his feet for as long as possible. More relaxed than he'd been in ages, he drove home and made love to his wife.

Chapter 18

After a busy morning shopping for new clothes, Saul drove Azize straight home, missing out on the lunch she had hoped for. Then, he showered, donned his suit and dashed to the office for an important meeting.

Azize removed the clothes from their packaging, throwing them in a pile to wash and dry before the next day when Saul would set off for London for a few nights for the GYP launch. She knew he was adept at bluffing, appearing more confident and in control than he was. But, she noticed the signs of nervousness, how he retreated into his cave and got edgy with those around him, particularly her. What should have been a pleasant morning choosing his new clothes had turned out to be a stressful exercise as he kept griping and looking at his watch. As always, when Saul took out his stress on Azize, she tried to find the right balance, aware that it wasn't personal but refusing to be a punch ball in the name of being supportive.

Saul arrived home earlier than usual. As soon as he finished dinner, he retreated to his study to prepare for the rigours that would begin tomorrow: a succession of briefings and interviews. Everything was happening so fast, with very little time to prepare, and the schedule was due to last for at least two-three weeks. He had wanted this role and was flattered that the board had considered him the best man for the job. He was confident enough in his abilities but concerned that there was minimal preparation time.

It was three-thirty by the time he got to bed. Creeping into the bedroom, he could make out the outline of his new suit, shirt and tie hanging on the wardrobe, the garment bag on the chair next to his overnight bag and polished shoes. He smiled. Knowing how busy he was, Azize had relieved him of the burden of packing. She was the best wife, he thought as she moaned restlessly in her sleep. He crept into bed beside her, trying not to wake her.

The sound of the alarm came all too soon, groaning and stretching to ease his stiffness as he climbed out of bed, feeling as though he had barely slept. He looked at Azize enviously as she lay there, still sleeping. She woke to the smell of Saul's new aftershave, which was too potent for the early morning and made her nose twitch. She sat up, noticing how pristine he looked in his new clothes. He came to kiss her, and she wished him luck, then watched him collecting his bags, wondering when she would see him next. She was feeling rough after another restless night. The recent events in London and the lady's fall had set her back to the degree that she feared closing her eyes in fear of her mind conjuring unwanted imagery of bodies lying in the road, but even when she slept, she sometimes had nightmares, usually to do with accidents of various kinds. She knew Saul too had been restless, which was understandable as his brain was awash with thoughts about the challenges ahead. She had an hour and a half before she needed to get up for work, finding herself drifting back to sleep and then sleeping through the alarm, flapping when she realised she only had twenty minutes to get ready. There was no time for a shower or breakfast. She quickly dressed, grabbed an apple for the journey, and forced herself outside. She had her medications in her bag but couldn't take them

on an empty stomach. After closing the front door behind her, she stopped in her tracks. She couldn't do this: she felt queasy and anxious. 'Deep breath!' she said out loud, then started walking as she concentrated on breathing. 'What if?' her mind said: 'What if this or that happens?' Her most esteemed therapist, Annie's dulcet tones echoed in her mind: 'Ground yourself! Focus on where you are. Feel your feet on the ground. Don't forget to breathe!'
'Garden! Bird! Road! Traffic! Dog barking! Man whistling!' she said as she forced her legs to keep walking. Her racing heart made her feel vacant and faint. 'Slow down your breathing,' she thought as she reached the bus stop in the nick of time as the bus arrived.
Jessie, the receptionist, looked up from behind her desk, noticing that Azize seemed flustered when she arrived and asked if she was okay. Her agoraphobia wasn't something Azize was proud of, and she kept it from her colleagues. Saul, Phoebe, and her close friend Lucy were the only ones who knew about it. Azize felt flushed as she explained how she had overslept and narrowly missed her bus.
'Well, you're here now. By the way, we're off to the Cat's Hat to celebrate my birthday on Saturday. You coming?' Jessie asked.
'Yes, of course, I'd love to.'
'Things have been stressful lately with Ian being off sick, so it'll do us all good to have a social. I think the last one was at Christmas.'
'I'll be there!' Azize chirped as she headed for the bathroom to get changed and take her medication.

***

Seeing Saul on television for his first interview filled Azize with pride with a tad of nervousness on his behalf. He looked dashing in his new charcoal grey suit, sky blue shirt, and navy polka dot tie, and she was satisfied they had chosen well. But she wasn't as convinced about his hair, wondering who had coaxed him into getting it cut that short. Nevertheless, he appeared confident as he sat on a sofa opposite Angela Beyrin. A brief wave of jealousy came over Azize as Angela introduced him when Saul gave her his best cheeky smile, and she, dressed in a red, tight-fitting dress, shifted her legs flirtatiously towards him.

Carmen was glued to the screen when Marta came in the room asking for something to eat. Carmen shooed her away crossly, telling her to ask her mother, fixing her eyes back on the television as the interview began.

'So, Saul, you are here to tell us about the GYP project. Can you tell us what it is exactly and why it is called the Global Youth Promise?' Angela began.

Saul smiled confidently as the camera zoomed in on him. 'Yes, the GYP is the first of its kind. It is a global enterprise that will bring under-privileged children and youths from as young as eight up to the age of sixteen from all around the world to the UK to compete in a range of sporting events. It will open up opportunities for them that could be life-changing.'

'How does the selection process work, and what do you mean exactly by under-privileged?'

'Well, to begin with, we will contact the governments to see who is interested in participating in the scheme, after which we will send out teams to discuss the terms and provide guidance. Then, it will be up to them to put the candidates forward.

By under-privileged, we mean children primarily from poor backgrounds whose parents can't afford to send them to extracurricular sporting activities, private clubs, or individual tuition. There are talented kids everywhere whose potential will sadly never be met. We want to change that to give children a chance. That is why it is called the Global Youth Promise: this is *our* promise to *them*.' As the PR team had instructed, Saul placed special emphasis on the last sentence, as it was to be their catchphrase. He smiled at the rapturous applause.

Azize beamed, delighted that everything was going so well so far.

Holding up a fist to the television, Carmen was seething. 'Since when did you care about children?' she cried.

'What is the ultimate goal?' Angela asked.

'We want to show children that anything is possible, that despite all odds, they can make something of their lives, and of course, to boost their confidence. And the ones who excel might get talent spotted, which could lead to a bright future. If nothing else, even travelling to another country is an experience, and they will make new friends and be seen on television worldwide. But not only that; united in its cause, a global project like this can help bring countries together.' Saul felt his nerves ameliorating as the audience burst into applause again. All the hours spent diligently studying and rehearsing were paying off. He shifted in his chair and looked at Angela intently, saying, 'That is not all.'

Angela cocked her head to one side. 'Really?'

'Yes, after this, we have other ambitions. We aim to make GYP an annual event introducing other projects in consecutive years: art, music, dance, inventions—you name it; the prospects are endless. We promise to open the door of opportunity to as many children as possible.' He smiled. He was particularly proud of this part since it was his own idea and he had managed to get Troyman Trust on board.

Angela leaned forward. 'But isn't this a Troyman Trust initiative? Where does Orion Enterprise fit in?'

'Orion Enterprise has seventy-five years of experience organising major events: anything from conferences to celebrity weddings to galas, sporting events, you name it. We have the expertise to drive this forward for the Troyman Trust. We are a coalition, and together we will do everything necessary to bring success to this important venture.'

'So, I imagine you'll be expecting a huge response of potential candidates, but how can you fairly judge one contestant over another? And what will you say to those who don't make it?'

'Well, obviously, there has to be a limit.'

'And what *is* that limit?' Angela cut in.

Saul shifted in his chair. 'The finer detail hasn't been decided yet.'

Like a lioness waiting patiently to surprise her prey, Angela made her move. 'Why not?' she asked pointedly. 'You are marketing the event, so you must have some indication of numbers; I mean, one hundred, five hundred, more?'

Azize yelled at the television screen, 'For crying out loud!'

Carmen couldn't hold back her laughter. 'Go, Angela, go! Make the smug git squirm,' she said, then frowned at Catalina for bringing Marta in, dressed in her pyjamas, ready for bed. 'Don't interrupt!' she said.

'Don't you want to take your daughter to bed?' Catalina asked frostily as Marta wrapped her arms around her legs.

'Yes, yes; you take her up, and I'll be there in a minute!' Carmen replied, her eyes never leaving the television screen as she spoke.

Catalina sulkily picked up Marta and left the room.

Carmen scrutinised Saul as he adroitly masked his feelings, beaming his magic smile at Angela and taking her off-guard. 'Like I said, it's early days, so all the details will be discussed and announced in good time. Now, can I get to your other question?'

Feeling slightly annoyed, Angela nodded. Azize clasped her hands together. 'Well done, Saul!'

'There will, of course, be a coordinated selection process, and the decision-making will need to be rigorous, but everything possible will be done to ensure that the right candidates are selected for the process.'

'But, inevitably, there will be casualties—disappointed young people subjected to false hope and rejection. That isn't exactly a *kind* promise, is it?'

Azize, who knew Saul so well, noticed the subtle clues that his mask was beginning to slip: minor tell-tale signs like fiddling with his wedding ring, tapping his feet and shifting in his chair. She bit her lip as she watched him throw up his hands. 'Obviously, we can't help the entire world's children, but we promise to provide the opportunity to as many as possible. Do you not think the focus should be on the positive rather than the negative?' he asked masterfully, gaining enthusiastic applause from the studio audience. Another goal to Saul!

'The slimy toad!' Carmen said through clenched teeth. 'Butter wouldn't melt in his mouth. He's good at putting on the charm, but it's fake; all fake!'

'Yes! Well done, Saul!' cried Azize, while Carmen stared blankly at the television, waiting for Angela's reply.

'Yes, of course,' she said. 'But no matter how you frame it, there are going to be a lot of children who will feel let down.'

'I'm afraid, Angela, we don't live in a perfect world, and I don't have all the answers, but we intend to bring children together from around the world with a promise of a brighter future. That is our aim and is what we are going to do.'

Time had run out, and the interview was brought to a close, making a quick switch to an advert break. Saul removed his microphone and looked up at Angela, sipping orange juice as the make-up artist hovered over her with her powder and brush.

'Thanks for coming,' she said impassively to Saul.

'You gave me a run for my money!'

'That's my job,' she replied as an assistant came to usher Saul swiftly away in favour of the next guest.

Saul was relieved it was over and received a string of congratulatory messages. What surprised him most was Ed calling to praise him for doing an exemplary job. He checked his schedule sheet. The taxi was due in forty minutes to take him to his radio interview. He went to the cafe next to the television studios and bought himself a sandwich and coffee. He read a message from Azize saying how proud she was, and one from Emma, short and to the point as always, saying: 'Well done, boss.'

The radio interview, lasting only ten minutes, was a lot easier. To Saul, it was an anti-climax, as Al, the presenter, enjoyed the sound of his own voice more than his guests. But, overall, he managed to get his point across. The final assignment of the day was the press release announcement, along with Troyman Trusts' Jack Brealson, taking place at four thirty, so he just had enough time to change his shirt in the toilets and freshen up, then grab another coffee before the taxi came to pick him up.

As the taxi arrived at Saul's hotel, he was exhausted but happy. It had been a whirlwind of a day, but all had gone swimmingly well, better than he expected, and the congratulatory messages kept coming. 'I was so proud of how you handled Angela Beyrin,' Azize told him when he spoke to her. 'She's notorious for trying to trip her guests up. What was she like in person?'

'Yeah, well, I was ready for her. She's quite sly: all nicey-nicey on set, but as soon as it's over, dismissive, like, okay, goodbye, and onto the next.'

'Yes, she seems up herself.'

'I would say a man-hater. She's the type who will flirt with a man, but if he shows an interest, quick as daylight, he'll be cast right back in the river.'

Azize thought it was a strange observation to make. 'Did she flirt with *you* then?'

'Me? I was too nervous to notice.'

'And yet, you looked so calm.'

'Like a swan, no one could see me quivering beneath the surface,' he chuckled.

'Will you be home this weekend?'

Saul looked around the hotel room where he would stay for the rest of the week. 'Yes. I should be home Friday night, all being well.'

'It's Jessie's birthday on Saturday, and we're all going to the Cat's Hat for a meal.'

There was a pause at the other end. 'Oh, I was looking forward to spending some quiet time together.'

'I know, me too, but I'll make sure I'm not late.'

'What do you mean? Aren't I invited?'

'No. It's a staff do,' Azize said, wondering why he made her feel guilty.

'It's not exactly well timed is it, not after the last couple of weeks, I thought you'd want to spend time with me.'

'Of course I do, but I'll only be gone for a couple of hours.'

'Okay, fine,' he hung up.

He looked at Azize's picture on his phone screen. With dark wavy hair and shy eyes, she was still beautiful, so other men must find her attractive. He wondered about Andrew, the dentist, who got to spend more time with her than Saul actually did. Zia was always talking about him, and he was apparently in the process of separating from his wife. Would he make a play for Zia? Would she succumb to his charms? Or was Saul being paranoid? Like most men who love their wives, he had jealous tendencies, but now they seemed more intense. Was it Shakespeare who said, suspicion always haunts the guilty mind? He couldn't bear to lose Zia, and it was time for him to step up, be a better husband and stop taking her for granted.

His thoughts returned to the cloud still hovering over his head, threatening to destroy everything he had. Despite his recent successes, there was still the issue of Carmen. She was like a persistent fly that, no matter how hard he tried, he was incapable of swatting. He was aware of the risks in asking for a DNA test. Would she set out to prove that he *was* Marta's father? He found it interesting how angry she had been when he asked for a DNA test. Was there a real possibility that she slept with someone else when they were seeing each other? Yes. Carmen craved male attention and was angry that Saul refused to leave Zia, so she might have done it to spite him. Saul wished he could erase the past, but all he could do was live in the hope that the truth would never reveal its ugly head, that he could put everything behind him: and that his secrets would remain hidden and buried for the rest of time. He had learned from his mistakes and was praying for a reprieve.

Azize looked at her phone, perplexed and annoyed about Saul hanging up on her. She didn't have much of a social life and felt resentful that she had to put up with Saul gallivanting about everywhere, but he didn't like it when, on the odd occasion, she wanted to go out. Was it that he wanted to spend time with her or because he didn't trust her? He had made several derogatory comments about Andrew lately, even though he barely knew him. Sure, she got along well with Andrew, but never in her marriage had she contemplated crossing the line. If anyone should be concerned about trust issues, it was her because Saul was away such a lot, and she had no way of knowing what he got up to. She wondered how she would feel if she discovered he had been unfaithful, the notion being too dreadful to contemplate.

She was determined to stick to her guns, but instead of getting out the begging bowl to ask Saul to drive her to the Cat's Hat, she would ask Jessie. To take her mind off things, she rang Phoebe to apprise her of her dad's recent acclaim to fame.

Chapter 19

With her mother out shopping and Marta at the nursery, Carmen was glad to have some space. The television in the background was getting on her nerves, so she turned it off. She needed some quiet time to think. Then, Julia burst in with the hoover. 'Upstairs first, please!' Carmen barked. On many occasions, Julie wanted to answer back, but she needed the job, so she kept her swear words to herself. She turned obediently and left the room without a word.

No longer did Carmen have love or happy families on her mind when it came to Saul. He had played the card she never thought he would; his coup-de-gras. She wondered why, after all this time, he decided to question his paternity. Of course, she couldn't prove he was the father because he wasn't. So, not only did it mean he would never have a place in their lives as she had planned, it also meant that she had to stop deluding herself that he held any affection for her. Now, Marta would be left without a father and a decent education. Carmen would have to forego her pension and would not be privy to the lifestyle she had planned; that she felt she deserved. All this because of the lies and deceit of a despicable man. He had betrayed her, and she would do everything in her power to make him pay. He may have played checkmate in the last game of chess, but Carmen had a plan which would out-smart Saul Curtis and was far deadlier than chess. She had the poison arrow that would destroy him.

Chapter 20

'It's good seeing you in such a good mood for a change,' Azize said as Saul bounced down the stairs in his dressing gown singing. He went to the drinks cabinet to top up his glass.
'You'll regret it in the morning,' Azize laughed.
'What the heck! We're celebrating!' he said.
Azize held up her glass to chink with his. 'Here's to yet another successful week!'
Saul didn't need reminding of the next round of media schedule. 'I need to get it all out of my head this weekend,' he said.
'I get it,' Azize replied. 'But don't forget we're out for lunch tomorrow. I know how you are with a hangover.'
Saul grimaced. 'You're right as always. I'll make this the last. Do you want to dine out twice in one day? I mean, wouldn't you rather cosy up with me tomorrow night and watch a film?'
'Saul, please don't keep griping on about tomorrow night,' she pleaded. 'You go out with colleagues all the time, all over the world. I never know what you're up to, but do I get on your back?'
'That sounds like an accusation. Are you saying that you don't trust me?' Saul asked defensively.
'No. What I am saying is that I know that socialising is an important part of your work, and I put up with it without interrogating you as you are me.'
'Put up with it, so you *don't* trust me?'

'Look, Saul, you're twisting my words because you're drunk. Of course, I trust you, and I'm offended that you don't seem to trust me!'

Saul's head was beginning to spin as he swirled the remainder of his whisky around in the glass before gulping it down. Azize looked at him, feeling disappointed that drinking so much so quickly meant that he would soon be asleep and snoring. She had been looking forward to celebrating his week's work with him, but now it was beginning to look like another lonely evening.

***

Even though Jessie was picking Azize up, she still needed to perform her exercises before leaving the house, which she did in the bedroom while Saul was downstairs. She saw her relapse as a weakness that left her both disappointed and ashamed. Saul thought her condition had improved because she was too proud to tell him the truth.

Saul sulked when she left. He was a hypocrite, but he knew what men were like and didn't trust Andrew. And dressed in a royal blue blouse and black trousers, Azize looked stunning. She also had makeup on, which was unusual for her. Who was she trying to impress? Saul wondered sullenly. He had honoured his promise to take her out to lunch but wasn't good company because of his hangover. He tried reasoning with himself that Zia had never given him a reason not to trust her. However, he knew from experience how easy it was to have your head turned, along with the temptations of flirting with someone who showed you attention, one thing leading to another. But not everyone is like me, Saul thought. He had taken advantage of his status as a successful businessman, which, to many women, was like bees to honey. Unfortunately, it had taken Carmen's threats to ruin his marriage to wake him up to realise what it meant to him, with a dread of losing it. He tried reassuring himself that Azize had a strict moral code, but he would not be able to relax until she got home.

On arriving at the restaurant, Azize found herself surrounded by inquiring colleagues about Saul's recent claim to fame, hoping to hear some inside gossip. But Saul had primed her on the importance of discretion, so rather than put her foot in it, however disappointing, she gave very little away.

Being a group of fifteen, the dentist crew was designated a side room. In all honesty, Azize would rather be at home cuddling up with Saul and watching a film, but she didn't want to ostracise herself by being anti-social, and she wanted to make a point to Saul. It was usually her at home alone while he was out in some city somewhere, living it up with his colleagues. It annoyed her that he didn't seem to trust her because she had never given him any reason not to.

Once seated, Azize quickly checked her phone, seeing three messages from Saul. Looking around, she noticed that others were also checking theirs. She found it rather sad that everyone was so dependent on them these days. Will, the most senior dentist at the head of the table, must have noticed it too, prompting him to hammer on the table to get people's attention.

'To honour this special occasion, may I propose a phone ban at the table?' he said. Most nodded in agreement, turning their phones off, although there were a few cursory mumbles from younger members, and Anne, one of the hygienists, refused because her babysitter might need to contact her. Just then, as if by divine timing, Azize's phone pinged. She apologised, turning it off and putting it in her bag.

Azize enjoyed the evening that passed by quickly, but Saul was moody when she got home because she had ignored his messages.

'What has got into you?' she asked crossly. 'You never used to be like this.'

'Well, what if something happened?' he complained. 'I mean, with your agoraphobia being so unpredictable, I worry about you.' He thought he was clever by turning it around from jealousy to concern for her well-being, but it didn't convince Azize.

'Saul, have I ever bothered you at work when I had a panic attack?' she asked.

'No.'

'You have no idea what I go through. I don't tell you the half of it, but I have learned to deal with it.'

Saul realised how selfish he had been, obsessed as he was with his own tribulations. 'I apologise. I've been taking my stress out on you lately.'

'Yes, we've both been looking forward to this weekend, and all we seem to have done is argue,' Azize replied. 'It's during these stressful times that we need to get on, to support each other. Don't forget your new role has an impact on me too. Everything is a lot easier if we are allies.'

Saul stretched out his arms, and Azize nestled into them. He kissed the top of her head and stroked her hair, saying, 'I'm so lucky to have you.'

On Sunday, they woke to bright sunlight poking through the gap in the curtains. After breakfast, Azize went out to do some gardening while Saul did some preparation for his forthcoming schedule, first in Paris, then onto Rome. As they enjoyed their sandwich lunch in the garden, Saul thought how peaceful it was here, birds singing, the trickle from the fountain into the small pond. He gazed at the pear tree, the bed of roses in early bloom of different shades of pink, the hollyhocks, carnations and geraniums. The garden looked good, all courtesy of his wife. Gardening didn't interest him, his sole contribution being to mow the lawn, but lately, he hadn't even had the time to manage that, so Azize had to do it. He raised his glass of home-made lemonade. 'It looks good!' he said. 'I see the forecast is fine for next week. I wish I could be here with you to enjoy it.' But they both knew it was a cursory remark because he would get bored soon enough. Even so, there was a part of him that meant it, that envied people who found pleasure in the quiet, who enjoyed silent moments, whereas he had to keep busy, on the move, always seeking a new destination, a new project. He closed his eyes to the world, enjoying the warmth of the sun on his head, a light breeze caressing his face. When he thought about it, any enjoyment he gained from his jet-setting lifestyle was usually short-lived, and his life was exhausting. It was soulless, he thought. Could the adrenaline rush of a fast-paced lifestyle be wearing off? Like the affairs, he had come to the realisation that the juice wasn't worth the squeeze. Saul never found the time or inclination for contemplation, but the tranquillity of the garden and the company of his wife in a precious moment yielded a portentous awakening. Metaphorically speaking, it was as though his soul reached out to him, yearning for peace. Was it time to stop climbing the mountain to admire the view? Saul Curtis was changing.

His reflection was interrupted by Azize asking how he felt about the week ahead.

'You know me, I'm schizophrenic. I'm chomping at the bit and simultaneously full of dread. It's my lot, Zia. It's the way I am.'

She smiled, raising her glass. 'Well, onward and upward, as they say!'

'Indeed! Onward and upward.'

Chapter 21

As she was getting ready for work, Azize received a call from Jessie, asking if she would cover for Tiffany, who, yet again, had phoned in sick. It meant working a full day rather than her usual half-day Monday stint. She looked at her watch, realising she needed to make a pack up for lunch, but had very little time. She tossed a few items into a bag and took her meds. She was resentful that she still needed them, telling herself they were a temporary solution, that no way on this planet would she allow herself to become dependent on them again.

When she arrived at work, Jessie looked at her awkwardly from behind the desk. 'It was a great night!' Azize said breezily.

'Yes, it was,' Jessie replied.

'Are you okay?' Azize asked quizzically, observing that she didn't appear to be her normal self.

'Yes, fine,' Jessie replied, but something was off. And Azize observed a strange atmosphere among her colleagues throughout the morning.

Jessie was in the restroom when Azize came in for her lunch break. She hesitated, wondering if she should tell her. Azize noticed her look of uncertainty, thinking she was upset about something. 'Come on, Jess, spit it out! You know you can confide in me,' she said.

'Actually, it isn't about me,' Jessie replied. 'You don't know about it, do you?'
Azize was confused. 'Know what?'
'What's in the news.'
'I tend not to watch the news as it's always depressing. Why, what has happened?' Azize imagined some terrible disaster, an earthquake, a mass shooting—
Jessie shook her head. 'I have to get back,' she said, going over to the bin to dispose of her rubbish. 'Just check the news,' she said as she walked out.
Azize took out her phone and went straight to the newsfeed. As she scrolled down, she froze when she saw a picture of Saul and Angela Beyrin, the headline boldly stating: *Saul Curtis, frontman of the GYP project is a fraud, claims his mistress.*
'What the—?' she gasped, bringing her hand to her mouth. She read on: *Saul boasts about the virtues of helping children with the Global Youth Promise but has turned his back on his own daughter, claims Carmen Sanchez. Saul, who is married, had a liaison with Ms Sanchez, resulting in the birth of their daughter, but flatly refuses to support either, leaving them destitute despite him being a very wealthy man. Knowing what he is really like, Carmen said she felt ill when she saw Saul on national television portraying himself as a benevolent force wanting to help the children.*
Azize felt faint, her head spinning, her heart beating like a drum. Jessie, stricken with a guilty conscience, returned to check on her. As she walked in, she noticed Azize's shocked expression, pale face, and her hands were trembling. She went to sit by her side. 'Azize, are you okay?'
Just then, Anne strolled in. Jessie looked up at her, asking, 'Can you get her some water?'

Anne went to the water machine. 'What's up, Azize?' she asked.
'I— I don't feel well.'
Anne looked at Azize, then turned her attention to Jessie, saying decisively: 'Cancel my appointments for the next hour and a half. I'll take her home.'

Chapter 22

When Anne turned into Marigold Lane, Azize saw several cars parked along the roadside near her driveway and a gathering of people with camera equipment and microphones. 'God!' she exclaimed.

'Is this to do with the news about your husband?' Anne asked.

Azize was feeling dazed and confused. 'I don't know. I suppose it must be,' she replied, even though everything seemed nonsensical to her right now.

'Do you have a back entrance?'

'Yes, turn there onto Bluebell Park Road.' She sank in her seat to avoid being spotted by the press, although she doubted they would know what she looked like.

Anne threw Azize a quick look. 'Are you okay?'

Azize felt ashamed for causing a scene and disrupting everything at work. Anne knew about the scandal, and Jessie would put the episode down to that: but her colleagues weren't aware of her agoraphobia, and blaming her sudden sickness on a news story, would seem disproportionate, so she lied. 'I've been feeling off all morning,' she said. 'I think I have a fever. I'm so sorry about this.' She indicated where Anne should stop, and they pulled up alongside the curb, with Anne keeping the engine running. 'Don't worry. We'll sort something out,' Anne said. I'll tell Andrew you won't be back for the rest of the week.'

'Thanks, Anne,' Azize smiled faintly, then looked behind to see if the press might have followed them, but all was clear. 'Do you want to come in for a drink?' she asked as she climbed out of the car.

'No, I have to get back. My advice is not to engage with the press. You take care, okay?' Azize waited for Anne to turn the car around, then waved her off. She opened the garden gate oblivious to her surroundings, not even noticing the sweet scent of the roses. Then she experienced a moment of panic when she couldn't find her keys as her shaking hands scrambled through her bag. But when she checked again, she found them lying at the bottom. She let herself in, marched through the kitchen into the living room and collapsed in a chair.

Azize stared at the wall for several empty moments, then took her phone out of her bag. There were several missed calls from Saul and a message in capital letters: *DON'T BELIEVE WHAT YOU READ IN THE PRESS!*

***

The taxi pulled up outside the Hotel Du Barry, and Saul climbed in the back. He slumped in his seat, his back aching from muscular tension, his face flushed with rage. In the state he was in, he had no idea how he would manage to focus on the tasks ahead. The first destination was the town hall to meet Pierre Germain, the Mayor of Paris, followed by the press conference precisely two hours later. He jolted at the sound of his phone's ringtone, his heart racing when he saw it was Azize. 'What on earth is going on?' she blasted. 'I can explain. Just don't believe it, okay?' Saul said impatiently. Then, he saw another call coming in from Ed. 'Look, I have to go.

I'll catch you later.' He ended the call, quickly switching to receive Ed's. He wiped his sweating brow. 'Yes, Ed?'

The voice at the other end was abrupt. 'You're booked on the four o'clock flight. A taxi will be at Gatwick to pick you up and bring you straight to the office. You'll find the details in an email.' He hung up. Saul flinched nervously from a shock wave.

Chapter 23

Azize's head was in a whirl, feeling the need to speak to someone. She rang Lucy.

'Yes, I saw it, love. I honestly don't know what to say. Have you spoken to Saul?'

'Briefly, but he denied it, saying it's all lies. Carmen Sanchez is a witch. Do you remember her? She was the one who tried to break up our engagement.'

'Yes, I do,' Lucy replied. 'Isn't she a bit of a nutter?'

'She dated Saul before I came along, and she seemed obsessive. I thought we'd seen the back of her and can't believe she's back in our lives again.'

'But, she's probably lying.'

'She says she has Saul's child, Lucy! Surely, she wouldn't lie about that!' Azize said angrily. 'I can't believe Saul would do this to me.'

'Well, I'd wait to hear his side before drawing conclusions. Some will say anything for attention. You see it all the time, people coming out of the woodwork to profit from someone they knew in their distant past.'

But as hard as she tried to reassure her, Azize couldn't help but think there was no smoke without fire. Her mind was a jumble of emotions, disbelief, confusion and anger, but until she knew the truth, she found it impossible to settle or focus on anything. She felt trapped in her home, forced to pull the blinds across to avoid being seen by the press standing in the street like a pack of hounds gathering for a hunt. Were they waiting for Saul to come home or perhaps hoping to get an interview with her? Unlike Carmen, Azize wasn't one for the limelight: she was Mrs Ordinary, wanting to be left alone to get on with her life, this being her worst nightmare. Saul wasn't due to return until the weekend, but she sent him a terse message warning him about the press and to use the rear entrance.

***

After Ed's call, Saul knew it was game over. He had spent the entire plane journey trying to figure out how to crawl out of the hole he had dug for himself. He felt he was on trial to defend himself against two of the most prized things in his life, his job and Azize. He entered Ed's office a defeated man, flopping into the chair, tired, pale and dishevelled. Ed, tight-lipped, looked up at him. 'How did this happen, Saul?' he asked unceremoniously.
Saul threw up his hands in a helpless gesture. 'Yes, I screwed her. You all know that anyway. But this paternity thing is nonsense. Carmen is a bunny boiler who is out to destroy me. That's the simple truth. What else can I say?'
'I suppose you must know how this reflects on the company.'
'Yes, I am gutted,' Saul replied.
'The board held an emergency meeting this morning, and I fear it is bad news.'
Saul looked him in the eye. 'You're withdrawing my role as publicity officer?'
'I'm afraid it's worse than that. Suffice to say we will accept your resignation.'

Saul felt the hackles rising on his neck. He had hoped for a ticking off, that the PR team would find a strategy to get everything back on an even keel. Despite so many years of commitment and dedication, despite an exemplary record, despite being an asset in the company, because of a stupid fling, he was about to be disposed of like a filthy nappy tossed in the bin. He laughed cynically. 'Huh! Oh, I get it. You want me to volunteer, and if I choose not to, I'll be pushed: that's how it works, right?'

'Business is ruthless,' said Ed.

'It's unlawful. I'll sue the company!' Saul protested.

'Ah, come on, Saul. You know better than that. Orion's legal team would eat you for breakfast.'

Feeling like a cornered rat, Saul felt that Ed secretly enjoyed witnessing his despair. He smiled weakly. 'When?'

'When, what?' Ed asked perplexedly.

'When do you want me to finish?'

'Well, now, of course.'

'Oh great! How charming of you!' Saul rose to his feet in anger.

'Calm down, Saul, please. The media intervention has given us little choice. God only knows why they are making a meal out of this: either they are using it to cover up some political issue or scandal, or there is nothing else to report. Either way, it is what it is, and we have a meeting with Jack in forty minutes from now. We have to be seen to be taking decisive action.'

'Let me be there! I can explain everything,' but Ed was shaking his head.

'But what about Paris and Rome?' Saul asked incredulously. He couldn't believe this was happening.

'Mike is on a plane to Paris as we speak. We had to implement damage control as quickly as possible.'

Saul frowned, clenching his fists. As if things weren't already bad enough, the news that Mike Benton, a cocky bit of trash, would replace him was an even greater blow to the solar plexus. He looked up at Ed with a puzzled expression. 'Mike Benton? Really? What experience has he got?' He slammed his fist on the desk out of frustration. 'This is ridiculous, Ed. All of this because of a lying bitch! At least allow me to fight my corner and give *my* side of the story. I've put my heart and soul into the company for years: Orion at least owes me that.'

Ed was a hard-edged man who had no scruples about firing Saul because he didn't like him much: but more because of how he had humiliated the company. But, putting that and his personal feelings aside, he couldn't deny that Saul Curtis had done a lot for the company, and men like him were difficult to replace. The cut-throat corporate world allowed no room for sentimentality, and thanks to Saul, a lot was at stake. Affairs were risky business, but Saul was a fool. Ed, too, had an affair many years ago, which put an end to the marriage. But that was a blessing in disguise because one year later, he met Lizzie, with whom he was happier than he'd ever been. 'Saul, this is tough, but you brought it on yourself,' he said. 'We all know what Carmen is like. Surely you knew you were playing with fire?' He glanced at his watch. 'I'm afraid the company is only concerned with business,' he said. 'It's brutal, but it's a fact, and *you* screwed up.' He stood up indicating the meeting was over, offering his arm to shake hands. But Saul ignored the gesture, turning his back on Ed as he headed for the door, then, determined to have the last word, he said: 'Have I ever told you you're a bastard?' Ed shrugged and looked at his watch. Now, he had to focus on the meeting with Jack.

Chapter 24

Still reeling from the bombshell of losing his job, Saul steeled himself for the next volcano to face at home. As far as Azize was aware, he was still in Paris, so he considered staying in a hotel for a couple of nights while things calmed down, but he knew it would be wrong; that he had to strike while the iron was hot, to speak to Azize, however hard it was going to be. He was glad it was a working day for her, so he had time to prepare himself for the onslaught. It was a hot day, and his clothes were sweaty. He needed a shower and a stiff drink in the garden to capture his thoughts before facing the music. Azize had warned him about the press pack outside their house, but he was surprised to see they were still there. Thank God for tinted windows, he thought as eager eyes stared at the car, following its passage. He swore as he turned into Bluebell Park Lane, parking out the back, slamming the door with the realisation that everything was spiralling out of control, escalating from a disaster to an unmitigated cataclysm.

Saul was met with another surprise as he strode into the living room and saw Azize on the sofa, a box of tissues, an empty wine glass, and a mug half-full of coffee on the table next to her. She looked dreadful, still in her dressing gown, her hair a mess, and her eyes red from crying. She started, equally surprised to be seeing him.

Saul's heart sank when he saw how pitiful she looked, all because of him. He ran his hand through his hair, groaning: 'What a godawful mess! I feel like I've been hit by a truck!' The sympathy card usually worked, but Azize was very guarded. She didn't show it, but seeing him in such a sorry state, his hair unkempt, the new shirt ruffled, no tie and bloodshot eyes; all played on Azize's empathetic nature, wanting to reach out to him, but she couldn't allow herself. She wanted to believe that Carmen had made it all up, that it was some sick joke, but she wasn't that naive to believe he was innocent. She awkwardly remained silent as Saul slumped in a chair, placing his hand on his forehead. 'My head is pounding!' he exclaimed. He looked up at Azize, knowing he was in for a rough ride.

Realising he was playing the sympathy card after all he had put her through, Azize felt a rising anger. 'Is the child yours?' she fired at him. 'When did that woman return to your life?' She couldn't find it in her to utter her name. 'She claims she's had your child. Have you been lying to me all these years? Has our entire marriage been a sham? Tell me the truth, Saul.'

'I bumped into her a few years ago quite by chance—'

Azize laughed. 'Huh! Nothing *she* does is by chance. Haven't you learned that one by now?'

'Just let me explain!' Saul replied crossly. 'When I saw her, she seemed depressed and was desperate for a job. As it happened, there was a temporary position at Orion, so I helped her out.'

Azize laughed again. 'You helped her! You know nothing about women, do you, Saul? Even now, you don't realise how manipulative that woman is. She played you for a fool. But then, it wasn't just a job you helped her with, was it? You threw in some sex for good measure, which was what she planned. You played into her hands, you idiot!' Her eyes were stinging with angry tears, but she was determined to hold it all together.

Saul had thought long and hard about what to say but knew he wouldn't get away with a blanket denial. 'I made a mistake!' he said defensively. 'It was merely a one-night stand after too much drinking when we were in—Paris. She was upset about something, and I consoled her, and then, well, one thing led to another. But, it meant nothing, just a one-off, a foolish, idiotic mistake.' He looked at his wife's swollen eyes and pale face, trying his best to be sincere, saying: 'I am so sorry.'

Azize felt numb and brittle. She took a deep breath. 'And the child? You had a child by her?'

'No!' Saul announced firmly. 'No, that is a lie.'

'How do you know?'

'Because the timing is wrong,' he lied. 'The kid is three years old, and the fling happened—'

'How do you know she is three?' Azize threw back sharply. 'You've obviously spoken to her about this. There was no mention of the child's age in the news article, at least not the one I read.' She raised her voice. 'Have you seen the damn press out there? How are we going to go out? This thing is a nightmare, Saul. So, tell me, how do you know the age of this girl?'

'Because—because she tried to blackmail me.'

'Oh?'

Saul hadn't planned on telling her any of this. 'Carmen was involved in a car accident and had no one to look after her daughter. She needed someone to mind her overnight before her mother arrived from Spain.'

Azize laughed cynically. 'This is getting better by the minute. I suppose that was the night of your emergency summons to Paris?'

Saul nodded, impressed at her deduction. He felt ashamed as the lies were accruing, one after another.

'Why didn't you tell me any of this?' Azize cried.

'I tried to protect you because I didn't want you upset. Honestly, the kid is nothing like me,' he protested. 'I told her to prove it with a DNA test, and she refuses, which, to me, is evidence of her guilt.'

'Whether it is true or not, the whole world has heard about it now!' Azize exclaimed. She looked at Saul, burying his head in his hands. 'I knew something was up as you've been very secretive lately. Are there any other revelations; because if there are, you had better tell me now.'

Saul hesitated, then said. 'London.'

Azize looked surprised. 'What about London?'

'I bumped into Carmen.'

Azize shook her head in dismay and disgust. 'Another coincidence, I suppose?'

'She stalked us, which is why I disappeared that afternoon.'

'Oh, good God! I knew the story you gave was false,' Azize said.

Saul looked up sheepishly. 'I'm sorry I lied to you. Carmen was there waiting when I came out of the toilets. She said she wanted me to sign something about the kid. I refused, and then she tried blackmailing me, threatening to tell you everything. I had to make a snap decision, but I didn't want to hurt you, especially on your birthday.'

Azize paused as the truth sank in, then replied sullenly: 'Well, it ended up being ruined anyway.'

'I know. Her hotel was right next door, and she promised it would take just a few minutes, but when we got there, Carmen drugged me.'

Azize was shocked. 'What? God, Saul, this is serious! You should have told me! We should have gone to the police.' At this revelation, her fury shifted more towards Carmen. 'I always said she was a crackpot!'

'She is, Zia! That's what I'm trying to get across to you. The woman is dangerous. She's even cost me my job!'

'Your job?'

'Yes, Ed sacked me this morning. I can't blame them because the scandal is causing detriment to the image of the company. I know I'm not blameless in this, but that woman is out to destroy me.' His voice broke, and Saul struggled to hold back the tears but failed. Azize couldn't bear it. If she had a weakness, it was seeing men cry. There was no denying he had betrayed her, but Azize knew how clever and persuasive Carmen was, and if he was telling the truth, the consequences of his actions seemed to outweigh the crime. She put her arm around his shoulder but held back from being overly sympathetic.

'I'm sorry, Zia, so sorry,' Saul choked. Azize handed him some tissues. She wanted to believe his side of the story that it had just been a one-off quickie, but it seemed unlikely. Whatever Carmen had done, he was still guilty of betraying her, and Azize wasn't ready to forgive. 'I'm going to have to sit on this for a while,' she said. 'I think we both need to.'

Saul looked at her with dewy eyes. 'What do you suggest?'

'Can you go to your brothers or somewhere for a few days?'

'What about you? How are you going to deal with the paparazzi outside?'

'I'll use the back entrance. Anyway, I won't be going to work for the rest of the week. I've taken the week off.'

Without another word, Saul rose from the chair. His bag in the car boot was full of clothes that needed washing, but the hotel would have a laundry service. Quiet as a mouse, he picked up the keys and walked out the back door.

Chapter 25

Carmen heard a hammering at the door. Catalina entered the living room crossly with her hands on her hips. 'I'm not answering. It's him!' she said petulantly. She had argued with Carmen about her going to the press, hailing it reckless and foolish, asserting it had brought even more disgrace to the Sanchez family. But Carmen had no regrets because Saul had treated her appallingly and deserved everything coming his way. Nonetheless, she hadn't anticipated all the media attention, which was beginning to get on her nerves.

Saul was in a turbulent mood, hammering on the door with his fist to vent all his pent-up anger and frustration. Perhaps it was just as well no one was answering as, in his unbridled state, who knew what might happen.

A hand tapped him on the shoulder, causing him to jolt. He turned suddenly as a young reporter thrust a microphone in his face. Behind, was a cameraman filming. 'Mr Curtis, is there any truth in Mrs Sanchez's allegations?' the reporter asked. Like a tormented bull, Saul robustly pushed past him for a hasty retreat, unwittingly knocking the microphone out of his hands. 'You'll be paying for that!' the reporter called out as he bent down to pick it up.

'Well, you shouldn't be here, should you? This is private property!' Saul yelled, resisting an urge to go back to punch the reporter. He headed for his car, but various journalists gathered around him, firing questions amid the sound of camera clicks. Just then, a police car pulled up that had been alerted by angry neighbours about the press corp disturbing the peace. Two burly police officers stepped out, and a red-suited woman marched straight towards them. At recent briefings for the GYP project, Saul learned that a breach of the peace was not a criminal offence yet held the power of arrest. Unless the press was causing a disturbance, they were not breaking the law, so in these instances, the police would usually ask them to move on.

Saul pushed through the small gathering to his car and climbed in. He was about to fire up the engine when a police officer bent down to the window, asking him to get out of his car. Perplexed and angry, Saul opened the door and saw the reporter in the red suit standing behind the policeman, smirking.

Saul's head was spinning as the policeman was reeling off a monologue of rehearsed jargon about his rights and telling him he was under arrest for causing criminal damage to a microphone. A plethora of noisy people began retreating from their houses to see what all the commotion was about. 'But that's ridiculous!' Saul protested. 'It was an accident! It's their word against mine. You can't arrest me without any proof.'

The woman in red stepped forward. 'It was all caught on film, Mr Curtis. You deliberately knocked it out of the reporter's hands.' Saul felt like an animal trapped in a cage as everything seemed surreal, and when the policeman produced a set of handcuffs, he was in utter disbelief. He looked at the house, noticing Carmen and Catalina watching from behind the kitchen window. As he met Carmen's gaze, her eyes were full of disdain; next to her was her mother smiling.

Chapter 26

Finding herself caught in the media's deadly net, Azize became fixated on the news, even checking her phone when she woke in the night. There were still titbits about Carmen's revelations, but with no new material, the news seemed dominated by other stories, so it looked like things were dying down. She hadn't heard from her parents, presumably because Turkey had more important things to report in the news than the trivia and gossip that were an obsession in the UK. Neither had Phoebe seen any reports in Australia's mainstream media, but she came across a couple of online video creators covering the story, finding it unbelievable that her parents were in the news. Azize was grateful that she had her and a few close friends' support, but, as a private person, alongside her see-sawing emotions was a sense of profound embarrassment. In a state of confusion, she was doing her best to keep a handle on things whilst trying to figure out who to believe, Carmen or Saul.

After emerging from a shower, she got a message from Lucy alerting her to turn on the news. She rushed down the stairs in her bathrobe and hair turban to turn the television on. She recoiled in shock at the footage of Saul being handcuffed and taken away in a police car.

***

Carmen was in a fit of laughter, watching a replay of Saul's humiliation on the TV with her mother. But, while she enjoyed watching Saul receive his comeuppance, Catalina was tight-lipped, believing now more than ever that her daughter had taken things too far. 'You got your revenge, but don't you see, *we* are paying too? Now we are trapped in this house! Why didn't you go ahead with the DNA test and get as much out of him as possible? Make him pay that way!' But she knew how obsessed her daughter was with Saul and had all along suspected he might not actually be the father.

'Because I want to humiliate him for the way he treated me!' Carmen protested.

Catalina threw up her arms. 'Santo Dios! Don't you see what you have done? Doesn't it bother you that the media are plaguing us? What about Marta? How are we supposed to explain all this to her? How are we supposed to get her to nursery on Monday?'

'You don't need to bother because Molly is back tomorrow.' Carmen was relieved to be getting the childminder back as her mother was driving her up the wall. 'You can go back to Papá. I can manage now.' Catalina was relieved too. She had carried out her motherly duties but was itching to get back home.

Azize rang Emma, whose matter-of-fact outlook always seemed reassuring. But she appeared to be equally surprised at the latest developments because it was out of character for her former boss to get on the wrong side of the law. She asked Azize if she was okay.

'Not really. I can't believe what is happening!'

'Me neither.'

'I can't get hold of him on his phone. I expect the police have taken it off him. Did you know about any of this with Carmen?' Azize asked.

'Only that Carmen Sanchez is trouble, always has been,' Emma replied diplomatically. She wanted no more involvement in dealing with Saul's dirty laundry, but she felt sorry for Azize, silently vowing to support her as much as possible.

'Can you give me Carmen's address?' Azize asked.

As angry as she was with Saul, Emma felt that his reckoning seemed disproportionate, especially after so many consequences. Thus, her mood towards him had softened. She also felt remorseful for her part in unwittingly colluding behind Azize's back to protect Saul. Even this one deed would never make up for it. She gave her Carmen's address with a warning. 'Be careful; she can be ferocious in her temper.'

***

Saul stroked his unshaven chin, his eyes searching the depressing room with grey walls and the few items of furniture, a desk with three chairs, including the one he was sitting on. Someone had etched the name John on the desk, and the rest of it was badly scratched. He could hear voices, mainly male, doors opening and closing. How did things come to this, he wondered? It was the first time ever he had been in a police station, and he had no idea what to expect, but it was all a ridiculous waste of his time. The past few weeks had taught him a lot about the press and how they operate, but this cynical attempt to keep the Saul Curtis story alive was beyond ludicrous.

He replayed the scene repeatedly in his mind of jostling past the reporter. Indeed, he had been more aggressive than necessary, but he had to push past him because the reporter refused to budge. There were no two ways about it; it was an accident, but was that how it would appear on film? If not, how would he prove otherwise?

He checked his watch, tapping his feet impatiently. Police stations were like hospitals, he thought, where time seemed to have no meaning. He had spoken to his lawyer, who told him to say nothing until he arrived. That was two hours ago. Half an hour ago, a policewoman brought him a coffee in a paper cup that was tasteless and a ham sandwich with limp white bread, which he ate only out of boredom. He put his head in his hands, wondering if the lawyer would successfully get him out of this mess. He thought of Azize and wondered how she would react if she got wind of this. He had put her through the mill when she deserved none of this, all for a bit of sex on the side! He pondered over the recent tornado of events: being accosted in London, blackmailed, a succession of media interviews, losing his job and potentially his marriage, and now he was at a police station awaiting his fate. You couldn't make it up, he thought.

Chapter 27

Azize planned the exercise meticulously, getting up early to prepare herself for the unenviable but necessary task. Anticipating there might be paparazzi outside Carmen's house, she had on a blonde wig she'd worn to a fancy dress party years ago. Her sunglasses wouldn't look out of place as it was a sunny morning, and her Panama hat completed the disguise. Standing back from the mirror, she smiled at the prima donna looking back at her. In an endeavour to outmanoeuvre a potential anxiety attack, she tried convincing herself that she was playing a part in a movie, even giving herself a new name to match her new identity: Daisy Doe.

But the image alone wasn't enough to quell the nausea and sense of panic each time she thought about leaving the house. Even after taking her medication and performing the relaxation and focus exercises, she found herself faltering as she went to open the back door. Doubt entered her mind as she asked herself if she needed to do this, but Annie's voice echoed in her mind: 'You have to face fear in the eye to overcome it.' She raised her shoulders back and took a deep breath, then forced herself to frogmarch out the back door, down the garden path to the back gate, arriving just as her taxi pulled up. As she sat in the back, more of Annie's guidance came to mind: 'Praise yourself for every hurdle you overcome, however small.'

'Well done, Daisy Doe! You made it this far: so you can do the rest,' she whispered to herself as she gazed out the window.

As the taxi turned into the cul-de-sac, Minerva Lane, there was a commotion of people and their vehicles, so the driver had to reverse and park in the next street, agreeing to wait for her. Azize knew there was no going back, saying under her breath as she climbed out the car: 'Come on, Daisy Doe, you can do this!' She strode past the inquisitive crew, smiling broadly and swaggering her hips brazenly. As the journalists whispered amongst themselves, wondering who she might be, she strutted down the driveway of number 11 and rang the doorbell. Behind her, she heard a woman remark, 'I'm sure that's a wig.'

As she waited nervously for the door to open, Azize reminded herself why she was here, gathering strength with her anger. Carmen was her nemesis, who had done her darnedest to try and split her and Saul up. She tried hard when they were teenagers and is back making another attempt. She is like a stubborn stain in a carpet; no matter how hard you try to get rid of it, it will never disappear.

An older woman answered the door, taking her by surprise. For a brief moment, Azize wondered if she'd come to the wrong house, but she saw a resemblance in the woman, who had a Spanish look about her. 'Hi, I've come to see Carmen,' she said.

'Who are you?'

Azize briefly hesitated. For fear of being turned away and courting unwanted attention from the press, she brushed past Catalina. 'I'm sorry, but the press makes me nervous,' she said apologetically. Then she saw Carmen standing in the hallway dressed in a pair of casual slacks and a white t-shirt, her right arm in a sling. Azize felt a surge of heat rush to her head in anger. Staring at Carmen disdainfully, she removed her hat, sunglasses, and wig with melodramatic flair. Carmen's look of surprise morphed into a wry smile. 'Azize!' she said. 'Well, what a surprise!'

Catalina looked at her daughter inquisitively. 'Make us a coffee, will you?' Carmen asked her. Her mother frowned as she turned and headed for the kitchen. Carmen walked into the living room with Azize following on behind. 'Take a seat,' she said, but Azize refused. She wasn't here for a cosy chat.

'How is Saul?' Carmen asked in her clipped accent. 'Have you spoken to him since his arrest?' she sat in an armchair while Azize remained standing with her hands on her hips. 'Arrested all because of you!' she snapped.

'He was like an erupting volcano, trying to ram my door down. Then, he attacked a reporter. I saw it with my own eyes! Your husband needs to learn to control his temper!'

'He was in that state because of you! Your lies have caused all these problems!' Azize cried.

Carmen waved her finger at her patronisingly. 'No, no, no! He chose to sleep with me. He seeded our daughter and refuses to take responsibility for her!' She scowled at Azize. 'Do you think your husband is blameless in this? Do you actually know your husband?'

'Yes, I do. Saul is a man who foolishly allowed himself to become seduced by a calculating vindictive bitch! It happens all the time,' Azize said, her voice shaking with emotion. 'You lured him into your filthy web. *And*, you're a liar! You claim that Saul is the father and yet refuse to do a DNA test. Well; for all your scheming, Saul has no feelings for you, so you have wasted your time.' She wiped her sweaty brow as she felt her heart racing, surrendering to sitting as she felt herself become unsteady. Catalina entered the room with the coffee tray, placing it on the table and went to sit down, but Carmen stopped her in her tracks. 'Leave us to it!' she commanded. Catalina looked from one to the other sulkily, then left the room, but Azize suspected she was the type who would listen from behind the door. Carmen held back until she had left the room. It was as well that Catalina was flying back to Spain that night, as the tension between mother and daughter had reached a fever pitch.

Carmen stared at Azize coldly; her malice intensified after the mention of the DNA test; the chink in her armour poked. 'Your husband is a bastard!' she spat. 'Do you think I am the only one he's slept with? Men like Saul use women like commodities, then leave them. And women like you are fools for allowing them to do it!'

'And, who are you to take the moral high ground when you sleep with married men?' Azize cried.

Carmen narrowed her eyes. 'I went to the press because men like Saul and women like you both need teaching a lesson: him for doing it and you for putting up with it!' She noticed how pale Azize looked and her sweaty brow, feeling no sympathy, only disdain. She rolled her eyes. 'Dios mío! You are so naive, aren't you? I believe I know more about Saul than *you* do.' She laughed.

Her head pounding, Azize stood up, knowing it was time to leave. She pointed at Carmen. 'Just leave Saul alone!' she said. 'If not, mark my words; you will be hearing from the police!' With that, she left the room, marched past a grimacing Catalina, put her disguise back on in the hallway, and went out the front door as Daisy Doe. As she left, she heard Carmen call out: 'Send him my love, darling!'

Chapter 28

In a befuddled haze of despair accompanied by the relief of being free, Saul perched on the bed in his hotel room, wondering what to do. He needed to speak to someone but no longer knew who to trust. He scrolled through his phone messages. There were two missed calls from his brother, Daniel, but he would never count on him for support. There was no love between them: his only interest was sheer nosiness. Other than Emma, who had tried phoning the previous day when he was at the police station, there was nothing from any of his former colleagues. Of them all at the company, she was the only one who showed any loyalty.

'Hi boss!' she chirped.

'Just call me Saul since I am no longer your boss,' he replied sardonically.

'Ok, boss,' Emma replied, waiting for a chuckle or snide remark, but was met with silence. 'What's been going on? I can't believe Orion sacked you! You're no saint, but Carmen is vile. I've blocked her and want nothing more to do with her,' she went on.

'I wish I could just delete her from *my* life!' Saul said bitterly.

'Guess who has taken your place?' said Emma changing the subject.

'Mike.'

'You got it, dickhead himself! He's like a bull in a china shop trying to make his mark.'

'I believe it; pissing everywhere to stake his territory,' Saul replied sourly. 'Ed told me. He was on his way to Paris while I was on the return plane to meet my fate, to get fired! He's always been up Ed's arse, and they're golf buddies, which says it all, a pair of boring twats.'

Emma sighed. 'You have a lot to answer for.'

'I know.'

'The last time I saw you, you were dragged away in handcuffs for accosting a reporter. Since when did you transform into a beast, Mr Curtis?'

'Wait a minute. How did you know about that?'

'It was all over the television.'

'Shit!' In the whirlwind of the past forty-eight hours, Saul foolishly overlooked that the press would broadcast the footage. He ran his hand through his unkempt hair, wondering if things could get any worse.

'I take it you're out now?' said Emma.

'Yes, but I can't go home as Azize's thrown me out of the house.'

'Sorry to hear that, but I can't say I blame her.'

'No, neither can I.'

Emma could tell by the tone of his voice how dejected Saul was. Trying to lighten his mood, she quipped: 'You're famous now. How does it feel?'

'To avoid a torrent of swear words, I'd best sidestep the answer if you don't mind.'

'Where are you staying?'

'I have a room at the Swan. Care to join me later for a drink? I could do with some company.'

'Done! I'll be there at seven.'

As he hung up, he realised how lonely he felt—like he was drifting in a dingy, lost and alone in a vast ocean with nothing in sight other than sea and sky.

***

Aside from an elderly couple, the bar was empty. Saul was relieved because his sudden infamy played on his paranoia that he might be recognised. He had frequented the Swan as a teenager when it had been an in-place to go, but after several management transfers over the years, its current status was more of a guest house than a pub. It was an old building, but the modernisation had stripped it of its character. Nostalgia had brought Saul back here—memories of carefree times, getting drunk, and playing billiards with the lads: the future being an unknown landscape full of optimism. Looking around, he recalled with sadness how lively it had once been: the jukebox playing; laughter; spilt beer; taking the mickey out of Dave, who stupidly collected beer mats, nicking them at every pub. Upstairs were four bedrooms and a shared bathroom. As soon as Saul saw his room, he knew he wouldn't be staying for long.
Emma swung through the door, wearing baggy jeans and a navy t-shirt with the word 'Smile' printed across it. Saul smiled at her sense of humour, feeling reassured by her presence. She had always made it plain what she thought of his adulterous behaviour. However, she was still here as a friend, for which he was grateful. One lesson he had learned lately was that during adverse times, friends show their true colours, the true ones being few and far between. Saul went to order her a drink and a second pint for himself.

'Come on, Saul. Give me the gory details of your detainment and how you got off,' Emma said, beaming as she slurped the foam off the top of her beer.

'It was a god-awful nightmare. I went to Carmen's house to speak to her, but she didn't answer the door. The next thing I knew, a reporter shoved his microphone in my face, and I pushed past him, knocking it out of his hands. The police turned up and dragged me off to the cop shop because the press claimed I broke their mike, doing it on purpose. I waited three and a half hours for my lawyer in a room that stank of piss and puke. Thank god, there was footage showing how obtrusive the reporter was, and we could prove the damage was accidental rather than intent.'

'Huh! Funny, they didn't show that bit, only you being cuffed and escorted into the cop car. But at least something has gone your way.' She chuckled as she spilt beer on her t-shirt. 'You can't take me anywhere, can you? Anyway, you're not the only one to have problems. I have to put up with Mike Dickbrain. I'm telling you, he is such an arrogant tosser.'

'I'm sorry about that,' grinned Saul. 'I never thought they'd fire me, to be honest. One minute I was being praised for doing an excellent job, and the next, they kicked me out!'

'You'll find something else. You have a good reputation in the field, and now you've been on TV, you can capitalise on that.'

Saul nearly choked on his beer. 'What, for being a monstrous philanderer?' he said.

'The corporates will look beyond that and see you for your talents.'

'Right now, I have more important things to worry about, like my marriage. I don't think Zia will ever forgive me. She was brought up by her grandparents who were very religious.'

'Aren't those people supposed to be all-forgiving?'

'Yeah, right.'

'Well, if you're happy with her, why did you do it? Weren't you getting it at home?'

Saul shook his head. 'I don't know why. I've been a fool, and don't I feel it now? You know I compartmentalise stuff; I always have.'

'What do you mean?'

'Well, I've always viewed sex as a recreational activity.'

'You're not getting away with that, Mr. Curtis! It's time to admit it's an ego boost: and besides, dissociating sex from your home life still affects your wife, so that's bullshit. How would you feel if Azize did it to you, justifying it like you just did?'

Saul felt sheepish. Emma was right. He had to take responsibility without making excuses. 'I know, I've kidded myself, been too cocky, thought I was the bee's knees, and could get away with it.'

'You need to stop compartmentalising and start prioritising, starting with your marriage.'

Emma's straight talk was humbling. 'I know. Losing my job is one thing, but Zia is my rock. The prospect of losing her is just too painful.'

'Well, if you get another chance and she decides to take you back, don't screw up again!' Emma said firmly.

Saul looked Emma in the eye. 'I won't, Em; it isn't worth it.'

'Mum used to say if you learn from a mistake and don't repeat it, then it's a mistake no more. Have you contacted her since getting out of the nick?'

'No, not yet.'

'Well, I can't stay long, so make sure it's the first thing you do.'

Saul finished his pint. 'I will. Thanks, Em; you've helped a lot. I don't feel like I have a lot of friends right now. Can we stay in touch?'

'Absolutely, and I'll still be calling you boss, whether you like it or not!'

Chapter 29

Being a sun lover, one of the drawbacks of England was the sudden weather changes. Watching the tulip heads drooping from the force of lashing rain, Azize felt like one herself, helpless, cold, and battered. She had no regrets about confronting Carmen, something she needed to get off her chest, but it left her with even more doubts than before. She knew her for a liar, but was it true that she was not the only one Saul had slept with? It pained her to think about them together.

'How could he do this to me?' she asked the wall opposite. Had she fooled herself all these years that Saul loved her? Had they been living a lie? It is often said that men, unlike women, don't get emotionally attached to sex, but being intimate with another woman felt like a betrayal of the worst kind, prompting her to question herself. Was she not good enough for him? Was he bored with her? Or was it just animalistic opportunity or simply greed? She knew Carmen was clever and manipulative, and she wanted to believe Saul that it had only been a one-night stand, but what if there were others? She asked herself how she would manage on her own if they split up. Saul had always been her pillar of strength. Would she be able to remain in the house? She imagined packing up her belongings in boxes and then going around the house, looking at all the empty rooms. She would have to trade her part-time job for a full-time one. How would Phoebe feel?

Everyone always commented that they were a close couple. If he loved her as he professed to, why did he do it? Why, oh why? Could the answer be as simple as *because he could*?'

But then she was brought back again to her own secret. Was she any better for withholding the very thing that plagued her every day of her life? Hers was a lot more profound. She had killed someone, then driven away: from thereon, trying to forget, living her life as though nothing had happened. It was a paralysing fear rather than heartlessness that caused her to drive away, but it had been such a terrible error of judgement. Had she stopped the car and called an ambulance, that person might now be alive. She shivered at the image her mind conjured of the body on the road on that shadowy night. But she hadn't gotten away with it because she still had to live with herself, and her agoraphobia was there as a punishment, as a constant reminder. So, she was no angel to judge anyone else's behaviour. A fling with a temptress was nothing in comparison, and the consequences he was facing seemed merciless. Besides all that, she was conflicted. On the one hand, she was furious with Saul, but the part of her who had always loved him made her feel desperately sorry for what he was going through now.

Her thoughts coursed around her head for what seemed like hours. But as dusk settled in, not knowing what was happening, she found her concern for Saul was mounting. Where was he now, and what would happen to him? She checked the news, but nothing. So, when her phone rang, she was relieved it was him. 'Where are you?' she asked.

'I'm at the Swan.'

'Not the police station, then?'

'You heard?' Knowing that she didn't watch the news, Saul had naively hoped she hadn't heard about it so he could explain everything in his own words.

'I saw it in technicolour!' Azize exclaimed. 'It was breaking news. I saw you being hauled away by the police for accosting a reporter. What happened?'

'Well, I didn't accost him. That was a lie. I pushed past, and he dropped his microphone. Anyway, the film footage managed to prove it was an accident, so I got off.'

Azize paused. 'Come home, Saul.' As she said it, she knew it was her heart speaking and not her head.

'What?'

'Come home. Let's try and work through this.'

Saul felt his spirits rising like a helium balloon released from its gravitational pull. Azize would forgive him, and all was going to work out okay. He wasted no time packing his belongings, paying the bill, and racing home eagerly to embrace his wife.

Azize stood by the kitchen window, watching out for him, but when she noticed the back gate open, she felt unsure, wondering if she'd been rash in inviting him home and whether she was ready in her emotional state to deal with it. After all that he had been through, she wasn't surprised by his shoddy appearance as he made his way up the path with his overnight bag. She bit her lip nervously as he opened the door. Putting down his bag, he searched her eyes to gauge her mood.

'Hi,' she said, akin to how she would greet a stranger, leaving Saul disappointed, as he had expected a warmer reception with open arms or at least a smile. He realised he had been naive in his expectations and that things weren't about to run as smoothly as he had hoped.

Chapter 30

Carmen poured herself a large glass of wine in celebration as soon as Catalina left for the airport. Her constant whittling about Carmen's involvement with the media had ground her down: going on and on about how it reflected on the family, strict Catholics, and all that, blah blah blah. It wasn't just Carmen who was relieved to see Catalina go. Julia had found her interference with the housecleaning an irritation.

Carmen had a schizophrenic love-hate relationship with the paparazzi. They were a nuisance, but whilst she would never admit it, she was enjoying the attention. Despite what her mother said, she was convinced she'd done the right thing and would use the media again should the need arise. Before Saul's arrest, their interest had begun to wane, but now they were reassembling like vultures salivating over a feast.

With her arm in a sling, nothing was easy, and the one thing Carmen missed was her mother for all things relating to Marta. She had far more patience with her than she did. She had gotten her up and dressed, given her breakfast, made her lunch box, taken and collected her from school, made her tea, and read her bedtime stories. With Carmen unable to drive, Molly had agreed to do the nursery runs for her, but the press outside complicated matters. Catalina had managed to avoid them because she'd used the car parked on the driveway. But since Molly would be waiting in her car on the roadside, Carmen had to take Marta out to her. When the mob saw the front door open, they raced towards them, a female reporter thrusting a microphone under Carmen's nose. 'Have you heard from Mr Curtis?' she asked.

'You're on private property!' Carmen shouted. 'Go away!'

The reporter ignored her: 'Why didn't you let him in the other day?' Carmen brushed past her, pulling on Marta's hand to keep up, but she resisted, saying: 'Mummy, I'm scared.' Carmen picked her up and pushed past the press towards Molly's car. Molly sat looking nervous as Carmen strapped Marta into the back seat. She shut the door and tapped on the car as a signal to go. Then Carmen turned with hands on hips towards the press gathering, who were firing questions at her. 'Don't you have anything better to do?' she cried. 'I have no news for you. You are wasting your time. Go and do some proper reporting!'

She stormed indoors, closed the blinds in the kitchen to blank them out and collapsed in a chair. 'Damn you, Saul, this is all your fault!' she reeled off in Spanish. She had invested so much time and energy in him, but it all turned out to be a lost cause. He had lied to her, all those sweet nothings and promises in the bedroom, the gifts he wooed her with. But he never promised her the one thing she wanted, to divorce his wife. Were it not for Azize, Carmen was sure Saul would be here with her, raising Marta as his own. All she ever wanted was a family life, but it appeared not to be her destiny, and being a single parent was tough. Azize might think she has it all, she thought bitterly, but she lacked Saul's loyalty.

Carmen had always enjoyed the challenge of a married man, but she found it rare for them to leave their wives. Alan had, but his marriage was a disaster anyway, and he wasted his time because Carmen didn't want him. Saul was the only man she wanted, but he wanted to have his cake and eat it. It was incredible how men justified their affairs, some lying about the marriage being on its last legs, while others claimed to love their wives but were bored. Some said their wives had lost interest in sex, and there were the Sauls of this world who were driven by arrogance and a sense of entitlement to have whatever they wanted. The old adage of men's inadequacy in controlling animalistic urges no longer stuck, not here in the twenty-first century, and anyway, women these days were just as bad. Saul always refused to speak about Azize, so Carmen never knew the truth about the state of his marriage, but she suspected he loved his wife.

Of all the men Carmen could have, why was she so obsessed with Saul Curtis? She found it hard to explain: and it had taken her years to wake up and realise he was a wasted cause. She had tricked Alan into getting her pregnant because it hadn't worked with Saul. But Alan knew nothing about Marta because she dispensed with him as soon as she found out she was pregnant, going to Saul to announce that *he* was the father. He believed it at first, so what had changed? Approaching the press was a double-edged sword, but since Saul refused to play ball, vengeance was her only card left to play. Besides, didn't they say that hate was love's neighbour?

***

'Don't cry, love,' Azize said to Phoebe at the end of the phone. 'It will all work out in the wash.'
'I can't believe this has happened. It doesn't seem like Dad.'
'Do you want to speak to him?'
'No, not at the moment, not after how he treated you.'

Phoebe had always been a Daddy's girl, and the descent from his pedestal was deeply distressing to her.

Despite everything, Azize knew it wasn't helpful for Phoebe to turn against her father. 'There are always two sides,' she said.

'I'm sorry, Mum, but there's no excuse for betraying you like that. If it were Finn, he'd be straight out the door!'

Azize paused, realising it was what she had always said. 'I've learned that nothing is black and white in this world,' she replied. Emotional matters could never get resolved over the phone. Were Phoebe still living in England, they could have met up and comforted each other. Then, once things had settled, they might arrange a family pow-wow like in old times. As soon as Saul returned, she knew she had been too hasty inviting him home, that everything was still too raw to come to any compromise. As usual, she had gone in with both feet, following her heart and not her head, when they each needed more space to think about things.

Saul was taking time in the shower, purposefully affording them both a little more space to think about things. It was a relief to be back, but devoid of any warmth from Azize, it didn't feel like home. The warm glimmer of hope she offered him earlier seemed to have set to ice, and after several sleepless nights and nerves like a coiled spring, his bitterness was turning to anger. When he went downstairs in his dressing gown, Azize was on the sofa pretending to watch television. She looked up.

'Are we going to talk, then?' Saul asked a little edgily. Azize turned off the TV. 'Where do we start?'

'Wherever you like.'

'I went to see Carmen, and she told me there are others.'

Saul wasn't expecting this. Feeling exhausted and demoralised with a tension headache, he had no reserves to fight an inquisition, going on the offensive. 'That woman continues to spew her lies, and everyone, even you, is falling for it! I expect better from you, Azize!' he said accusingly.

His words caught her off-guard. There she was, expecting a grovelling apology, and instead, he batted the ball right back at her. 'How do you expect me to believe you when have already lied to me?' she cried.

'I don't because you believe that bitch over me, even though you know what a calculating liar she is!' He cupped his hands round his head to ease the pain, then threw them down theatrically. 'I don't see how this is going to work!'

Azize watched as he turned and marched back up the stairs, then ten minutes later, dressed in a pair of jeans and a t-shirt, left with his overnight bag without saying another word. She was perplexed, his anger and hostility capturing her unaware. Somehow, the tables had turned on her so that *she* felt like the guilty one. She chewed on a fingernail nervously while contemplating what went wrong. To begin with, she was foolish for inviting him to come home when their nerves were still in tatters: and rather than use diplomacy, she had allowed her feelings to get the better of her.

Saul drove to the Swan in a torrent. He was angry! Angry with Carmen, angry with Orion, angry with the media, angry with Azize, angry with himself. Sooner or later, he'd have to look for another job, but while this nightmare was going on, there was no chance of that. He would be receiving a good severance pay, but it was no consolation for losing a job he enjoyed: cast out like a criminal for the crime of having a fling. It was goddamn ridiculous.

The bar was busy when he arrived, with small groups at the tables, some chatting with others deep in thought, and then he realised it was a quiz night. As he self-consciously made his way towards the bar, he felt all eyes were on him, praying that he wouldn't be recognised. Rose looked up as she finished pulling a pint for a customer. 'Hello, love, you back?' she asked in a defined cockney accent. Saul suspected she might know who he was, especially as he had given his name for the booking, but she hadn't said anything.

'I'm going to need the room after all,' he said.

'That's alright, love. You paid for the week anyway. Let me finish with my customer; then I'll get the key.'

'And a pint of Heron, please,' said Saul. In the background, as the quizzers muttered amongst themselves, came the next question: 'What is the capital of Spain?'

Saul threw his bag down, removed his t-shirt and sat on the bed. He checked his phone, noticing several missed calls and messages, but he wasn't in the mood to look at them properly. Instead, he turned to the newsfeed, and saw the headline: *Carmen Sanchez's rage at the press*. There was an unflattering picture of her outside her house, displaying her fists. 'Is nothing else going on in the world?' he yelled, then he rang Ed.

'Hi, Saul. I was wondering how you were getting on?'

Saul wanted to vomit at his ex-bosses insincerity. 'What the heck is going on?' he demanded. 'Orion is keeping the story running for publicity. So much for firing me to make it go away: the PR team has changed tactics, now encouraging it as a cynical marketing ploy—and all at my expense!'

'Calm down, Saul!' Ed said in his patronising voice. 'I don't know what you're talking about. Why would Orion do that?'

'Because it's free PR for the GYP and Orion Enterprise, that's why. As the old adage goes, any publicity is good publicity, whether good or bad. I know how these things work.'

'It's not true.'

'Well, I don't believe you!' he hung up. Emma was the one who had told him about the rumour circulating at the company, and he believed it. Another news flash appeared on his phone. *Is this Saul Curtis's latest mistress?* He looked at the screen aghast, clicking to open the story, revealing a picture of him and Emma drinking pints together here at the Swan, with the caption: *Saul was seen with the mystery woman at the Swan Public House.*

Seeing red, Saul grabbed his bag and ran downstairs to the bar. All eyes were on him as he went to speak to Rose, who was busy polishing glasses. She looked up, noticing his angry face. 'Is everything alright, love?' she asked.

'No, it isn't!' Saul muttered crossly under his breath, trying his best not to draw too much attention from onlookers. He showed Rose the news story. 'What's this?' he asked. Rose calmly got her glasses out of her pocket and looked. 'Well, I don't know anything about it,' she said, shaking her head. 'It must have been one of our customers.'

'Yeah, right! In my memory, apart from an old couple, we were the only two here,' he replied. He threw the key on the counter and picked up his bag. 'You can stuff your room!' he said, and stormed out to his car.

Chapter 31

Azize felt shattered, deciding on an early night. When her phone rang, she thought it might be Saul apologising, but it was Emma, who, omitting any pleasantries, said concisely: 'Don't believe what you see on the news.'
Azize felt her heart skip a beat. 'Oh no, what now?'
'They're trying to make out that I'm having an affair with Saul.'
'What?'
'That's right. He asked me—'
Azize interrupted her. 'I can't stand any more of this. It's just too much,' she stammered.
'Can I come over?'
Azize hesitated. 'Yes,' she said.
'I'm on my way.'
Being night-time, it was unlikely, but just in case there was any press lurking around, Azize told her to use the rear entrance. While waiting for Emma, Jessie, the incumbent from work nominated to check on her, called. Azize didn't mention anything about the news, simply saying that she had a virus and hoped to be back soon. She dismissed Jessie's mention of sick notes, as she had far more important things on her mind.
Seeing Emma wearing a baggy t-shirt, jeans, and a baseball cap surprised her. The only occasions she had met her were at the odd work function when she dressed up: and when they spoke on the

phone, Emma's efficient manner projected an image of being crisp and sharp, probably wearing a suit. But this was the true take me as you will, Emma. Azize was nervous when she arrived, feeling unprepared for yet another bombshell. While she found it hard to comprehend that Saul had also had a fling with her, she no longer knew what to believe; besides, Emma had spent a lot more time with Saul than Azize.

Emma took off her cap as Azize apologised for being in her dressing gown. 'Can I get you a drink?' she asked.

'No thanks. I guess you know about the story?'

'Yes. I saw it on my phone.'

'Well, the truth is that Saul feels he doesn't have many friends right now, and he needed someone to talk to about everything, so we arranged to meet. That is all there is to it.'

Azize looked at Emma, whose sincerity shone through. She certainly was no Carmen. 'I believe you,' she said. 'This is all beyond ridiculous. I don't understand why the media is so obsessed with this non-story. They're making mountains out of molehills.'

'I agree. Some of us have our suspicions.'

'What do you mean?'

'Since Mike took over from Saul, we think he's deliberately exploiting the story for publicity.' She looked at Azize, who looked pale and confused. 'Let me explain,' she said. 'As publicity officer, he works closely with the PR team, who, in turn, are affiliated with journalists. It's how things work in the media world.'

'But it isn't exactly positive publicity, is it?'

'No, but it puts Orion Enterprise on the map.'

'How cynical! Saul isn't speaking to me, so I don't know what's happening. What did he say to you?' Azize asked.

'He is as low as anyone can be. Yes, he's an arse, and he knows he's been stupid, but he is remorseful. He's scared of losing you.'

While wanting to be reassured by Emma's words, he hadn't provided any evidence to her. 'You wouldn't know it. He won't talk to me, let alone apologise,' she said.

Emma shrugged. 'Men are useless at expressing their emotions. Carmen is the type who throws herself at men just for the sheer hell of it, an ego trip, and she has no scruples about who she sleeps with.'

'I know, but infidelity is a betrayal and hard to recover from. I went to see Carmen, and she told me there were others. Do you know if it's true?'

Emma paused, aware that her following words could hold a lot of sway over the future of the couple's relationship. She was a person of high integrity, but there were occasions when a slight untruth was kinder and wiser than a cruel truth.

'Not to my knowledge.' She shifted and leaned towards Azize. 'Look, I am no marriage counsellor, but we have choices in life, and we all make mistakes. You have to decide if your marriage is worth fighting for, and if it is, you need to talk to Saul and get it back on the road. You both look as though you're about to collapse.' She looked into Azize's tired eyes, saying earnestly: 'I don't know you very well, but I know Saul, and I like you both. Take it from me; you need each other.'

Azize wiped her moist eyes. 'You're right; none of us are perfect. We all have our secrets. Thank you, Emma. I'll think about what you said.'

When Emma left, Azize picked up her phone to ring Saul but stopped herself, deciding it would be best to sleep on it.

***

Feeling vulnerable about being recognised, Saul had no idea where to go. Having barely eaten for the past few days, he felt light-headed and needed a stiff drink to help him relax. Eventually, he pulled up at the Traveller's Rest Inn, a cheap off-road hotel. The receptionist appeared put out at the interruption as she tapped away on her phone, but at least she was too young to be interested in the news and barely even looked at him.

After dumping his bag in his room, Saul headed on foot to the nearest pub, just a few minutes away. The Trotter's Arms was in serious need of modernization. A pool table in the centre dominated the room; that had to be walked around to get to the bar. Saul found a small table in the corner. His paranoia was getting the better of him as he tried to keep his head down so as not to be recognised, though no one seemed to be the slightest bit interested in him. The first pint was very welcome, going down quickly. He went to the bar to order another, along with a whisky chaser, then decided he needed to eat, asking for the bar menu. After ordering a beef and ale pie and chips, a middle-aged man standing at the bar looked at Saul, asking with a broad smile: 'Are you the geezer I saw on the tele?' Saul focussed on sifting through his change to avoid eye contact. Then, he shrugged with a look of surprise. 'Not me,' he said dismissively, then returned to his table. When he sat down, he noticed the man and bar-man were watching him. From Saul Curtis anonymous a few weeks ago to Saul Curtis infamous. How did that happen? As he was checking his messages, his phone rang. His initial thought was Azize, but the number was unknown. He went outside to answer in privacy.

'Hi, Mr Curtis?'

'Who is this?' Saul asked suspiciously.

'It's Kit Barlow from Central News. We have an offer that you might well be interested in.'

Saul clenched his fists. 'Who gave you my number?'

Kit ignored him. 'We would like to offer you the opportunity to put your side of the story out there.'

'There *is* no story!' he barked, then hung up. How on earth did they get his number? He looked around to see if anyone was watching him, someone holding up their phone to take his picture to sell to the paps. There was a young couple flirting with each other at the wall and a couple of men smoking, none paying any attention to him. He blocked Central News on his phone, wondering if the several missed calls from unknown sources were also from the media. Henry, his lawyer, had advised him to keep his head low and avoid the press at all costs. He imagined how things would go if he were foolish enough to accept the offer from Central News. What would he say? He was guilty, after all: and in going public, god forbid, others could come forward like a load of hungry hyenas, looking for scraps of money and fame. What a nightmare that would turn into! He'd seen this kind of thing before in the media. Stories got exaggerated; women he had never met might even come out with falsehoods. He quickly flicked through his newsfeed, relieved at finding no more new stories to do with him. Hopefully, the whole thing would soon die down, although Henry had warned him to keep his wits about him, not to give into complacency and expect the unexpected.

As the alcohol mellowed his mind, Saul realised how shameful he had been to Azize. He walked out like a coward when he should have stayed to face the music. But when he thought about it, he was better off staying away from home because if the press found out he was there, not only could they make his life hell, but Azize

would become more of a target, and she had nothing to do with any of this. He scrolled through his messages again: a friend from the tennis club, his nosey brother, still none from Orion, except for Emma. He realised he should have rung her to apologise for inadvertently getting her involved in his mess, but with everything going on, it had escaped his mind. He read her message, accompanied by a series of angry emojis. 'Goal for them!'
He wrote back: 'Sorry!'
She replied with a comical emoji of a bearded man with spectacles, so typical of her sense of humour. 'Why? It isn't your fault. Are you ok?'
'Surviving.'
'Ride the wave'! she replied, including an emoji of a man swimming. Saul smiled. She was right: it was sink or swim time.
'Check out 'Victor's View' at ten for tosser Mike's five minutes of fame.'
Saul frowned. The thought of his usurper grabbing the limelight on television sickened him to the core, but he knew he had to watch it. He looked at his watch and saw he only had ten minutes, so finished his pint and went back to the hotel.
Victor's View had just started, and to a backdrop of emotional music, children from around the world of all colours and creeds, including some disabled, were depicted playing various forms of sport. Then the scene switched to the familiar studio, and the revved-up audience cheered as Jo Victor introduced Mike Benton. Saul felt a pit in his stomach. The GYP project was *his* baby, which he'd worked on for months with the team. What had Mike done? Nothing. And now, adoring the attention, he swaggers on stage, grinning like a Cheshire cat. That should be me, Saul thought bitterly. Mike, a true narcissist, was ruthlessly ambitious and played

the game well. The first thing he did when he started at Orion was invite Ed and his wife to a dinner party, also registering at the same golf club. Saul suspected his wife, Ali, as a greedy social climber, played a key role in his ambition. Saul frowned at Mike's smug grin and garish red tie, which clashed with his cropped red hair. It pained him, but he felt compelled to watch the man who had risen from his own ashes because something he had learned from this debacle was that he needed to keep one step ahead of the dangerous game.

In his renowned laid-back style, Jo Victor, wearing black-framed glasses, looked into the camera. 'Those of you who don't know about the Global Youth Promise Project by now must have been living under a rock!' He turned towards Mike. 'It's true, isn't it; the publicity around this event has been phenomenal?'

Saul frowned at Mike's supercilious grin on his freckled face. 'Indeed. It is the first of its kind; a mammoth task, but our children are our future, and not only does it open up the opportunity to the underprivileged, but it will bring countries around the world together in a unifying cause.' The audience clapped, but Saul knew Mike was merely quoting his briefing, and the interview came across as rehearsed and manufactured because, unlike Saul, Mike was wooden and devoid of charisma.

'What sports are involved?'

'Our focus is on individuals as opposed to teams.'

Saul grinned as he watched Mike use his fingers to reel off the sports in order to remember them all. 'Athletics, racket sports, swimming, martial arts, gymnastics, even skateboarding.' He smiled at the audience as they applauded. 'And,' he went on, 'we have plans for other projects in successive years.' Saul clenched his fists. 'That was *my* idea, dickhead!' he roared at the television.

'This is just the start of something major, and it isn't just for the children because it will create jobs. The possibilities are infinite,' he went on.

Saul couldn't bear to hear anymore and was about to turn off the TV when Jo said: 'There has been a lot of scandal around it all. How has all the noise about Saul Curtis affected things?'

Azize gulped, Carmen smiled, and Saul felt the tension rising in his body as they all waited for Mike to reply.

'We don't allow gossip to deflect us from the big picture. We keep our eyes fixed on the goal, which is the Global Youth Promise. It is that to which we devote all our attention.'

'Ah, but is it gossip?' Jo remarked cheekily, winking at the camera. 'Saul Curtis, do you know him?'

Mike shifted in his chair uncomfortably. 'No,' he lied. 'As I said, gossip holds no relevance.'

'Liar!' Saul shouted at the television. 'You don't know me, huh?' But what angered him the most was his last comment, as though Saul himself was no longer relevant. It was how Orion viewed it. After years of devotion, hard work and loyalty, they wiped him from history as though he had never existed.

Jo didn't want to let go. 'Do you know how he's doing now?'

'No,' Mike replied awkwardly, now struggling to keep his pleasant mask in place.

'What about Carmen Sanchez? Do you know *her*?'

Even though he had worked with her only briefly, Mike denied that too. Jo had nowhere else to go, so he turned the conversation back to the project, and Saul switched off the TV in disgust. As usual, the media tried to turn everything into a silicious scandal rather than focusing on the main topic.

Azize watched through to the end. Knowing how Saul detested Mike, she imagined he would be cursing at the screen.

Carmen laughed at Mike's denial of knowing her. 'Revenge, sweet revenge,' she said as she turned off the TV.

Chapter 32

Saul woke with a sore back after an uncomfortable night. The mattress was too soft, and his room backed onto a busy main road, so the sound of traffic was ever-present. He needed to curb his drinking, but presently, it was the only thing keeping him sane. He looked around the bland room. He was used to staying in hotels far classier than this and the Swan, but he resented paying a lot for what he hoped would be a temporary arrangement. He turned the thermostat down as the air felt dry and oppressive, and filled the kettle to make a cup of tea.

He thought about Zia, wondering how she was feeling. He wanted to contact her but wasn't sure how best to approach it. He waited until nine o'clock, then rang Emma.

'Yo, boss! I'm just about to go for my run. You okay?'

'Too much alcohol. My own fault, of course,' Saul replied.

'Did you see the programme?'

'Yes. Rubbish! He didn't say anything new; just wanted to rub it in for me and make his mark.'

'The company will regret putting him in your shoes. Hey, have you contacted Zia yet?'

'Not yet. Any tips?'

'Grovel! You have a lot of making up to do. But take things slowly. Don't swamp her.'

'Okay, Em, I'll let you get on with your run. Cheers.'

***

Azize heard the rain tapping against the window as she opened her eyes, feeling sluggish after another bad night. According to the clock, it was only 7 am, but it seemed pointless languishing in bed, so she got up. She was running low on food supplies and medication, but had been putting off going out. She dreaded returning to work tomorrow, not just getting there and back, but she was embarrassed about facing her colleagues. She even felt awkward talking to her friends. Her phone rang just as she was contemplating whether she'd get away with taking a few more days off work. It was Saul. Communication was stilted, but Azize's anger didn't stop her from caring. She wanted to know where he had stayed, what he had eaten, and how he had slept. Her interest gave Saul reassurance and a little hope. 'How about you?' he asked.
'Keeping my head above the parapet. Did you watch Victor's View last night?'
'Yeah: it was utter garbage!'
'Mike loves himself, doesn't he?'
'Oh yes, biggest ego on the planet.'
The casual conversation had a calming effect on Azize. Even though they both knew they were skirting around the issues, small talk seemed the right thing to do at this time. As the saying goes: small steps towards big goals. The fact they were talking at all was progress. 'What's next?' she asked.
'I'll be keeping my head down, and I suggest you do the same. It'll all fizzle out soon enough, but we shouldn't give the media any more ammunition.'

A part of Azize was in conflict, disappointed in one sense that he wasn't begging to come home but rationalising that neither of them was ready yet.

'Are the press hounding you? Are they still outside?' Saul asked.

'There are fewer now, but the diehards are still coming and going.'

'So, they haven't discovered the rear entrance?'

'No, thank God. I've been going out incognito, wearing my blonde wig.' She didn't tell him she'd only been out once this week.

'Clever girl! Are you back at work tomorrow?'

'Yes.'

'Look, Zia, I don't want you to think I don't want to come home—'

'I understand. It's too soon,' Azize replied.

'Not just that. It will cause more trouble if the press finds out. You've been through enough already.' It was dawning on him how selfish he had been, fixating too much on his own predicament. 'Look, I have been an arse, and I'm sorry. Are you sure you're alright?'

'I'll be better when things settle down, but, hey, it is what it is,' she replied.

As he hung up, he wondered if things could return to where they were before all this started. Azize was thinking the same thing. She still loved him, but since trust and loyalty had been comprised, was it enough?

Chapter 33

'Well, you know what you can do with your job!' Carmen yelled down the phone. Work was refusing to give her sick pay as she hadn't bothered sending in sick notes. 'I hate this country!' she shrieked after hanging up. Her nerves were on edge. The press hounded her day and night, and Marta was playing up after Catalina's departure, protesting about going to nursery. And now this. Her phone rang, and she answered quickly, hoping that it was Artemis having a change of heart after her threats of quitting. But she recognised the trilly voice on the other end straight away. 'No, Belinda, I am *not* interested in doing another article. I've told you that already. I am done with it all—finito!'

'I thought you might want the opportunity to reply to the recent allegations against you?'

'What allegations?'

'A woman called Lucia Martinez?'

Carmen's heart skipped a beat. 'Lucia Martinez? What allegations exactly?'

***

Azize's wig, sunglasses, coat and bag were lined up on the sofa, ready for work. She had left half an hour to go through her relaxation exercises to prime herself for leaving the house. When the phone rang, she first thought to ignore it, but when she saw it was Emma, she answered.

'Sorry it's early, but have you seen the news?' Emma asked.

'No. Oh no! What now?'

'A Spanish woman is doing the dirty on Carmen!' Emma was glad to be the first to present her with the joyful news.

'What do you mean?'

'I'm afraid I don't have much time, but you'll see it anyway.' With that, she hung up, then rang Saul, who was still in bed. He switched on the television and went straight to the news channel but saw nothing about it, eventually finding it on his phone app: *Carmen Sanchez, my best friend, stole my fiancé!* He read it quickly to get the gist of the story. Lucia Fernandez claimed several years ago to have been a close friend of Carmen's. But everything changed after she discovered her in bed with her fiancé, Mateo. Saul vaguely remembered Carmen telling him about it, citing it as her reason for coming to England. He should have heard alarm bells ringing at the time, he thought.

Lucia described Carmen as a ruthless predator: *She ruined our relationship and never apologised. We had to cancel the wedding and lost a lot of money over it. Not only that, but it destroyed the friendship between our families. Carmen doesn't care who she hurts. She is a woman to keep husbands away from at all costs.*

Finally, some good news, thought Saul. Carmen was getting her comeuppance. At the end of the day, he knew he had to take responsibility for the affair, but he prayed that this latest revelation might in some way help his cause with Azize. It was surprising that she was talking to him at all. It felt like progress, but there was still no guarantee that she would forgive him. But, knowing how these stories fed on themselves, the prospect of another woman he'd slept with stepping forward for her moment of fame haunted him. What if the genie was let out to reveal that he was a serial adulterer to the world? Not only would it put an end to their marriage, but it would also destroy his reputation. He imagined the headline: *How the mighty fall! The man who once had everything now has nothing.*

***

When Azize read the story, she empathised with Lucia, taking comfort in her words that she wasn't the only one afflicted by Carmen's poison. At last, a reprisal for Carmen getting a taste of her own medicine. Lucia was right about her assessment of Carmen. Azize recalled a humiliating scene in Trubury high street when they were both teenagers. Azize was coming out of what used to be Marion's Cafe, now the Cup and Saucer, when she saw Carmen storming towards her like a bull to a red flag. Her words still reverberated in her head: 'He's mine! You stole him from me! Saul is mine!' Whilst feeling excruciatingly embarrassed, Azize replied as calmly as she could: 'People are not commodities. You can't own them. Saul doesn't want you, and it's time to get over it.' She walked away, but Carmen, who had no boundaries, shouted a string of obscenities after her down the street. Back then, as a carefree teenager who had not yet been bridled with debilitating panic attacks, Azize found the experience embarrassing but also amusing. She viewed Carmen as immature and unhinged but would get over Saul and move on. Little did she know what was to come. Never would she have guessed that her dark obsession would return to haunt them years later. Carmen was what she was, but it did not excuse Saul's behaviour. He had chosen to sleep with her.

Nevertheless, news of Carmen's retribution smelled sweet. Perhaps there was justice in the world after all.

Chapter 34

Catalina was at the end of the phone. 'Have you seen the news?'
Carmen clenched her fists. 'Yes, Mother!'
'What are you going to do? Your father and I are beside ourselves. It's so humiliating. We don't know what to say. You had to bring it up again, didn't you? You have brought disgrace to the family.'
Finding it incredulous that the story had reached Spain, Carmen held the phone away to avoid her mother's shrieking.
'Lucia is a liar!' she replied. 'Mateo was going to end the relationship. Besides, why now, after all these years, is she whining about it? She's doing it for the money.'
'You knew the wedding was all planned. They had everything arranged, then it had to be cancelled, all because of you.'
'Because of me? Why is it always *my* fault? Mateo was the one who was engaged. Are you trying to tell me that he was innocent in all this? She had a lucky escape if you ask me.'
'It's always about *you*, isn't it? You don't care about our relationship with Lucia's parents, do you? You have no idea how long it took for Mariana and Pedro to speak to us again after that. And now, the past is being stirred up again.'
Carmen raised her eyes to the ceiling. She had hated living in Spain, in a village where everyone knew every man's business. Growing up, the Sanchez and Fernandez families had always been close. She recalled Mariana arriving at their house in tears and the yelling

match that ensued. But had that not happened, she wouldn't have gotten on a plane to England. She would never have met Saul, and her life would have taken a completely different course. But Carmen believed in fate and that she was destined to meet Saul. She still believed that things hadn't gone the way they were meant to, that they were supposed to be together, but Saul had used his stubborn free will to resist, believing he was happily married when he evidently wasn't, or he wouldn't sleep around.

She found it hard to believe how the story had escalated. When she had approached the press, never in a million years did she think the news would reach Spain. There was no point in pursuing this conversation as Catalina just talked over her, so she hung up. Hearing the familiar sentimental music, she glanced at the television commercial showing an array of children's smiling faces. Then came the obnoxious voice-over: *The children are our future. The Global Youth Promise pledges to unite the world in a common cause. This is OUR promise to THEM.* 'It's everywhere, and I'm sick of it!' Carmen cried, hurling her phone across the room, which, lucky for her, landed on the sofa.

Chapter 35

Saul rubbed his eyes as he sat up in bed and turned on the TV to blot out the incessant noise of traffic, a constant drone of engines. What was there to get up for? There was no job to go to, and he longed for the comfort of his home and wife, but that, too, was out of bounds. Just a couple of months ago, he had had it all, and now he was all alone in a cheap hotel room. The only small mercy was his severance pay, but he needed to find another job before he went round the bend. In terms of fulfilment, pay, bonuses and the various perks, Orion was a hard match to follow. Dejected as he was, he realised there was no point moping around, so after indulging in a full English breakfast at the cafe next door, he spent some time revamping his CV and registering with a couple of executive agencies.

Emma rang as he was closing his laptop. He felt uplifted by her voice, grinning as she still insisted on calling him boss.

'Hi Em, how's it going?'

'Don't ask! Things are kicking off here, fireworks an' all. I've just come out of an emergency meeting called by Troyman Trust.'

Saul was all ears. 'Tell me more.'

'They're upset about the hijacking of the GYP by the scum media. Jack is fuming that the focus on everything positive has become a hotbed of gossip. You could cut the atmosphere with a knife in the board room. Boy, was it entertaining watching Mike squirm as he tried to defend himself, blaming it all on the media. But Jack was having none of it. There's a rumour that Mike has been pocketing money for his part in it.'

'I wouldn't be surprised,' Saul said. 'If you feed the media with so much as a flicker of a flame, and they like it, it will quickly become an out-of-control forest fire, is what my lawyer said.'

'Exactly. The interesting thing was that Ed didn't try defending him, even though rumour has it that he too was in on the strategy. All along, he has been saying that publicity, good or bad, is key and the main objective. There's been some stuff going on between Jack and Ed, too, with Jack pointing the finger at him for firing you so rashly when, above all else, you were doing a great job. He believes the strategy was wrong and that the way to deal with the scandal was to ignore it and push the positive PR even harder. There is even talk of asking you back. Would you, if they asked?'

'In a heartbeat, but it will never happen. I know Ed too well. Trust me, he would do everything in his power to prevent it. Besides, there is far too much water under the bridge: the media would make a meal of it, and it would never work.'

'There are ways,' Emma replied. 'They would do their best to keep it all under wraps away from the media. Now that the press releases are over—'

Saul interrupted her. 'Emma, trust me, it won't be happening.'

'Huh! So I'm still lumbered with Mike.'

'He's still in the job then?'

'Yes, the consensus is that another replacement wouldn't look good.'

'From what I've seen, it's been overkill. Saturation puts people off. The advert is dreadful.'

'I agree. I imagine the entire world knows about it by now.'

'Yeah, well, trust me, Mike has played it wrong. It was my baby, Em, and I would have handled it completely differently.'
'Their loss, boss.'
'Mine too, unfortunately,' Saul replied. 'But before you say anything, it's my fault; I accept that.'
Emma sighed. 'Well, I hope you learned your lesson.'
'To be honest, it has put me off women, full-stop, although there are exceptions, of course, with the likes of you.'
'And Zia?'
'Yes, Zia, of course.'
'What's happening there?'
'We're having a cooling-off period.'
'Good idea. She needs space, but don't go ignoring her. She needs to know you care.'
'Yes, I know. How about you? Are you alright?'
'I'm just keeping my head down, trying to avoid arguments. There's so much friction, not just at Orion but Troyman Trust as well. They haven't given themselves enough time with the project. With only months to go, there are all sorts of problems, both politically and logistically, the main one being getting the kids over here. Then there are arguments about funding, with sponsors pulling out after all the adverse publicity.'
'Wow! It's probably a good thing I'm not there.'
'Trust me, if you were with us, the landscape would be entirely different.'
'Thanks for the compliment, but projects like this are never straightforward. I warned them that it was overoptimistic running it this year. I put my heart and soul into GYP, but right now, the one and only thing I care about is getting my marriage back on track.'

'I'm sure she'll come around; just don't rush things. At least Carmen is getting a taste of her own medicine with that Spanish woman speaking out. Let's hope it gets the ball rolling for others, so we can watch her get annihilated.'

'Yes, it was great,' Saul said. 'But, what if other women come forward to speak about me?'

'It would blow your chances of reconciling your marriage, I guess.'

'That's what I'm scared of, Em.'

'You have to keep everything crossed that this blows over and fast. Just hang onto your stations!'

Chapter 36

After her period of absence, Azize noticed a strange atmosphere at work. Apart from asking if she was feeling better, no one had mentioned anything about the stories in the media. No doubt they didn't know what to say, which, in a sense, was a relief, but the silence was deafening, and she wondered what they were saying about her behind her back.

Arriving at the garden gate after another busy day, she removed her hat and wig, and heard someone approaching from behind. It was Madge, her neighbour. 'Will you tell those pests to stop hanging around?' she shouted. 'They keep blocking our driveway. It's getting ridiculous now!'

Azize looked at Madge's pudgy red face with dark roots showing through her greasy hair. Madge and Derek were aggressive busybodies—the kind who look for trouble, whom Azize and Saul tried to avoid as much as possible. Last year, it was about the garden fence, and the year before, they complained about the noise during the reconstruction of their driveway.

'What do you expect me to do?' Azize asked.

'How should I know? It's your fault that they're here. Give them a story, or tell them to piss off. All the time you avoid them, they'll keep hanging around.'

'There's nothing I can do, Madge,' Azize replied, turning her back on her and starting down the garden path.

'If you don't, I'll tell 'em about your rear entrance!' Madge shouted after her. She only had one volume: loud.

'I wouldn't if I were you.'

'Don't tempt me!'

Azize shook her head crossly as she entered the kitchen, throwing her keys and bag on the table. All she wanted to do was sit down with a cup of tea after a hard day's work, but she couldn't take the risk of Madge carrying out her threat. She went to the front door and opened it. At the end of the driveway was a small gathering, fewer than previously, which was a good sign. She called out, asking if anyone wanted a cup of tea. A woman in a green skirt and cream blouse conferred with her colleagues and nodded: 'Four white, two with sugar, please.'

As Azize made her way towards them with the tray, she noticed Madge standing in her front garden with hands on her enormous hips, watching every move. At once, Azize came up against a barrage of questions. 'There's no point in asking me anything,' she said firmly. 'I have nothing to say. You are all wasting your time here and upsetting the neighbours, so please drink your tea and move on.'

'Where's Saul?' a woman asked, and it dawned on Azize that it was Saul they were after, not her, so she replied, 'He isn't here and will not be returning for quite a while.'

'Have you separated?' the woman quickly fired back. Azize had a sudden realisation. She should have kept her mouth firmly shut as she had intended, because now she had opened up fresh speculation for them to feast on. She decided to say no more, turning quickly on her heels as the press continued firing questions. She removed her shoes, pulled down the blinds, and made herself a mug of tea. Feeling tense, she wiped her clammy brow, noticing her hands trembling. She refrained from an impulse to trade her tea for a glass of wine, knowing how unwise it was, being on medication. She panicked when she couldn't find her pills. She'd taken them to work with her, but they weren't in her handbag. Eventually, she discovered they were in her jacket pocket.

Once she had calmed down, she rang Emma for advice about her blunder with the press. 'Saul will be furious if they make something of this. Do you think I should tell him?' Emma knew how fragile things were between them both, and like it or not, her middle name was now "mediator." 'Let me tell him,' she replied. 'But be prepared for more paps possibly arriving.'

'Oh, I hadn't thought of that!'

'If I were you, I'd go away for a few days just in case. Anyway, I'm afraid I have to dash. Everything's kicking off here at work. You lie low, okay?'

'Okay, thank you, Emma. I appreciate your support.'

Azize spent the next ten minutes flicking through the news stories, but so far, the only one doing the rounds was about Lucia Fernandez.

***

Saul was disturbed by Emma's news. He had wanted to keep Azize away from the mess and wasn't there to protect her. He rang to see if she was okay.

'Sort of. Has Emma spoken to you?' she replied.

'Yes. Look, shall I come home?'

'No, it's best you stay away, or the story could escalate. I'm sorry. I shouldn't have interacted with the paps, but I didn't know what else to do.'

'Well, none of us have a degree in ducking and diving the media. I'm worried about you. Can't you stay at Lucy's or something?'
'I thought about that. Lucy and Serena have both been brilliant, but the last thing I want to do is involve them, and I doubt they'd thank me either.'
'Well, come and join me at the hotel. It's a hovel, but I could find somewhere nicer?'
'But were we to be discovered, it would stir up a hornet's nest.'
'This is awful. I'm beginning to feel like a caged animal!' Saul complained bitterly.
'Me too.'
'Well, let's see what happens over the next few days. Orion is trying to steer the press away from the gossip.'
'How? It's impossible to stop a tidal wave, Saul.'
'I'm not sure how these things work, but I daresay money changing hands may play a part.'
'I just want this to be over.'
There was an uncomfortable pause, then Saul said, 'I miss you.'
Azize felt a quiver, saying faintly, 'me too.'
'I spoke to our lawyer, Henry, and his advice is to lay low and remain tight-lipped. I'll give you his number in case you need it.'
'It's a bit late giving me that advice,' Azize lamented. 'But I learned my lesson. Wit and good old-fashioned common sense are all that are needed.'
'I'm at the end of the phone if you need me.'
As she ended the call, Azize reflected on the irony that the consequences of what had driven them apart were now paradoxically bringing them together.
The next day, the news came in: *Where's Saul? Mrs Curtis claims they have separated.*

The headline left Carmen feeling excited. She tried calling Emma, but it just rang and rang. It was the third time she had tried, to no avail, and it was looking increasingly likely that she'd defected to Saul's camp. Swearing in Spanish, she hung up. Emma was no loss anyway. She'd only stayed in touch with her because of her connection to Saul.

***

Azize found herself waking up early every morning to check her phone for news, today being no exception. She wasn't too surprised to see news of yesterday's faux pas, but she was angry at how they had outrageously lied to make a story out of nothing. She messaged Saul to warn him, and he replied with a heart emoji. Soon after, a message came in from Emma with six happy face emojis on either side of a statement: *Keep calm and carry on!*

Finding it hard to get back to sleep as she lay there, Azize realised that Saul and Emma were both right about her moving out for a few days to avoid the media attention, not least because she couldn't trust Madge to keep her mouth shut about the rear entrance. She got up early to book a room online, pack an overnight bag, and then run through her exercises before putting on her disguise and leaving via the back door.

She encountered pandemonium when she opened up the back gate. In a maelstrom of noise and confusion, she was quickly surrounded by a gaggle of journalists all talking over one another. They thrust microphones at her, firing questions against the backdrop of clicking cameras. Her disguise managed to camouflage the terror she was feeling. She took a deep breath, silently telling herself she was her alter-ego, Daisy Doe: confident, carefree and a narcissist who thrived off the media attention. Somehow, as she pushed past those standing in her path, she conjured a false smile and swagger as she rushed down the road with her heavy bag on her shoulder. Her head was still pounding as she arrived at the bus stop. Hot from nervous perspiration, much to the surprise of others waiting in line, she removed her hat and wig.

But when she arrived at work, another surprise awaited her. Azize could tell something was wrong as Jessie looked up from behind the desk and told her sheepishly that Will wanted to speak to her. Azize felt uncomfortable, wondering what she'd done wrong. She parked her bag in the rest room, then went upstairs to Will's room. 'Ah, Azize, take a seat.' He closed the door and stood with his back to the cabinet as Azize perched herself sideways on the dentist chair. He watched her apologetically from his six-foot-three height. 'My name should be Frank because I don't beat about the bush,' he laughed, but rather than making her feel more comfortable, his words made her more nervous. 'I have no idea how you have managed to cope with the assault of publicity lately, and I want you to know we are here to support you,' he went on. Azize wanted to find his words reassuring, but she could sense a *but* coming. 'But we are concerned about the potential impact on the business should the media discover that you work here.'

Azize studied her nails nervously. 'Are you sacking me?' she asked timidly.

Will shook his head. 'We are in a dilemma,' he replied. 'You have done nothing wrong, so to do that would be both unethical and libellous. We also take into account how hard things are for you at the moment and feel that it would be best for all concerned for you to keep a low profile. We thought you might want to use some of your holiday leave?'

Azize looked up at him. 'I only have two weeks left. If things haven't died down after that, what then?'

Will smiled. 'Well, we can assess the situation again and see where we're at.'

Azize was disheartened. 'Saul has lost his job, and now I, too, am being punished.'

'I do hope you can see it from our point of view, Azize, because we have to put our clients' best interests at heart. Yes, it's an outside chance, but what if the press followed you here? What if they waited outside for you to leave? We can't allow our clients to be compromised.'

Azize had to accept that he was right. She went to collect her bag from the restroom and left the building. She had a room booked at the Happy Circumstance Hotel on the outskirts of town, but the booking-in time was 2 pm, and it was only ten to nine. What on earth would she do to kill time? In a daze, she walked down the high street to the Cup and Saucer cafe and ordered a latte: doing her best to distract her turbulent thoughts by studying the layers of milk and coffee, the froth covered with sprinkled cinnamon. It looked like a work of art too attractive to drink. She looked around at her fellow customers, wondering if anyone recognised her, telling herself it was unlikely, but word spread fast in these parts. She took a deep breath and tried to focus her thoughts. She needed to make some calls, first to ask if the hotel would accept her earlier, then re-arrange the time of collection with the taxi. She would also need to tell Saul about work, but couldn't face that yet. The earliest the hotel allowed her was noon, and she didn't want to carry her overnight bag around the shops with her, so she would need to spend as long as possible at the cafe. She thought about the last time she was here when she had bumped into Liz. Wait a minute, hadn't she said she'd seen Saul at her grandson's nursery? Now, armed with the knowledge that he had met his so-called daughter, she realised it was possible.

With time on her hands, she flicked through her phone messages. Lucy had tried calling, and there were texts from other friends. Saul had warned her not to speak to anyone, whoever they might be, not because they weren't to be trusted but because they could innocently say something to somebody else who could leak it to the press. Lucy had her own problems, and Azize didn't want to add her rejection to the list, so she sent her a message promising to call when she got the chance. She noticed a missed call from Phoebe. Azize had purposely left her out of the loop of the recent developments because she didn't want to worry her. She sent her a rambling message about everything, barring the elephant in the room, signing off by saying how busy things were but promising to get in touch soon.

There was another missed call, this time from her mother. Could she have gotten wind of the story in Turkey? It was possible, as these days people have apps on their phones that give them access to news from other countries. Thankfully, Phoebe didn't bother much with the news as she found it depressing. Azize tried to recall the last time she'd spoken to her mother, deciding it was about three months ago, so why now? Knowing her as she did, she was like Saul's brother, Daniel, whose motivation to get in touch would be out of sheer nosiness rather than empathy and support. Where were her parents when she needed them? Were they contacting her because of an overblown news story or out of genuine concern for a troubled daughter? Azize knew the truth, and it hurt. She had been brushing the matter of her parents' indifference under the carpet for far too long. As a child, she could never understand why they lived so far away, and no matter how loving her grandparents had been, those feelings of isolation remained with her to this day, highlighted even more after Saul's betrayal. The situation needed addressing but now was not the time. In the meantime, with enough on her plate already, she decided not to respond.

Time went by perilously slowly, and Azize tried to ignore the furtive looks from the waitresses, wondering why she was still there two hours later, so she decided to buy a sandwich and a lemonade, taking her time to eat. But as hard as she tried to distract herself by going through her phone, she had to face the harsh reality of her situation. Due to an act of deceit and indiscretion on Saul's part, they both found themselves jobless, thrust out of their home, devoid of friends, and living apart. Carmen was a wicked woman who had come from hell and was doing her best to drag Azize and Saul back there with her. But Saul knew what he was doing: lying and cheating, potentially destroying their marriage with his filthy secrets. But she reminded herself again that her secret was far worse. She was a murderer, so was no one to judge. Azize was beyond redemption, while Saul was being strung up for an act common to man.

Chapter 37

Paid for by the broadcasting company, Carmen arrived in a taxi at the London television studio, looking in awe at the expansive modern building. She headed towards the main entrance with her garment bag over one arm and the tote bag on her shoulder. Inside, the foyer was a vast space, the surroundings far too modern for her taste. She headed for reception, announcing that she had an appointment with Belinda Taylor, but the young receptionist informed her that Belinda was in a meeting. The clock on the wall was showing 12.10, so Carmen thought it was more likely that Belinda was on her lunch break. Having arranged to meet at 12.00, Carmen expected her to be there to greet her. Belinda had pursued her day after day for this interview, and now she didn't have the decency to turn up. Carmen wasn't impressed.
'How long will she be?' she asked.
The receptionist shrugged. 'I can't say, but there's a coffee machine over there. I'll send Belinda to you as soon as she gets here.'
Carmen walked towards a cluster of plastic seating upholstered in various bright colours. She looked around critically at the gauche modernity, a long way from what she had expected. In a place like this, there should be Chesterfield sofas, not cheap bucket chairs, she thought in disgust.
The interview was scheduled for a three o'clock start, so, taking into consideration there would be a briefing of some sort, and Carmen

needed to change, then get her hair and make-up done, there wasn't all that much time. She thought about Lucia Fernandez and how spiteful she'd been in coming forward to slur her name. She was here to show her, alongside defending her reputation. But, of course, she was also here to deliver her coup de gras to Saul Curtis. Why not take advantage of a bad situation and turn it into something lucrative? Besides, who knows where things might lead? Another fifteen minutes later, Carmen was mightily unimpressed, storming over to the receptionist, telling her that if Belinda didn't turn up in the next fifteen minutes, she would be off. The woman looked surprised but remained calm. 'Of course,' she said, but not wanting Carmen to be stood over her while making the call, she politely asked her to go and take a seat.

Ten minutes later, a flawlessly made-up young woman with immaculate hair in a fitted orange statement dress and peep-toe stilettos strode towards Carmen. 'Hi, I'm Deborah. I'm so sorry Belinda has been delayed, but if you'd like to follow me, I'll show you around, and we can get started on it all.' Carmen huffed, rolling her eyes, then followed Deborah, admiring how confidently she managed to stride in such precarious heels.

***

Azize's hotel room was a fair size, and the bed looked comfortable. There wasn't much of a view, but the hotel was at least on a quiet street. Whilst unpacking, Emma rang. 'Yo! Are you still at home?' she asked.

'No, I took your advice and am staying in a hotel.'

'Good decision. Well, there's something you'll want to watch tonight; nine o'clock, The Jo Show; yours truly is going to be interviewed.'

'Not Saul?'

'No, your nemesis.'

'Really?'

'Yep. It'll be amusing to see how Carmen Sanchez tries to convince everyone that she's an angel and not a slut!' Emma chuckled. 'The floodgates are open, and rumour has it other women may come out after that Lucia woman, so this is a desperate attempt to save herself.'

'I thought you were friends?'

'Not really. I came to realise that her reason for staying in touch had nothing to do with me; it was about Saul.'

'I can't stand much more of this, Emma. When will it end?'

'Orion and Troyman have brought in another PR firm to sort things out, so, with luck, sooner than you think.'

'I hope you're right.' She contemplated telling Emma about her job, but she might tell Saul, and it would sound better coming from her.' Unlike Emma, the news of tonight's interview deeply perturbed her. Would there be more revelations she didn't want to hear? She knew Carmen was a liar, so the struggle of who and what to believe would only bring more confusion. She contemplated not watching, but knew she had to. When Saul rang, he was furious to hear about her job. But she explained that she was partly relieved because she had relapsed and was finding it difficult getting to and from work. She also understood the reasoning behind it: and after all, it was only temporary.

'I'm glad you saw sense and moved out. I think it's time for us to be together now. I'm going to check in to your hotel,' Saul said.

'No, it's too soon. If we're spotted together—'
'I'll check in under an alias and stay in a separate room.'
'I want it, Saul; I do, but I don't think it's wise yet.' She changed the subject. 'Have you heard about tonight's interview?'
'Yes. Emma told me. God knows what lies will spill forth from her mouth. Whatever she says, Zia, don't believe her. She is capable of saying anything.'

Saul felt gutted when he hung up, cringing at the prospect of Carmen divulging more incendiary information. It was why he planned on watching it together, so that he would be in a position to defend himself. But, now, the best he could hope for was that it would be less damning than he predicted and the outside chance that Azize wouldn't believe her lies.

As though the day hadn't been bad enough, later that afternoon, another story appeared with a picture of Azize standing outside her back gate in her disguise and the headline: *Is this Azize Curtis?*

Chapter 38

Jo Waldorf introduced her guest to cheers from the audience. Azize was transfixed as she watched Carmen, tall and slim, in a stylish cream pantsuit with her right arm still in a sling, beaming at the camera as though she was a well-known celebrity. She took her place on a sofa with bold orange cushions while Jo, in a short blue dress, sat next to her in a chair. Between them was a glass-topped coffee table equipped with two glasses and a bottle of something, probably water. Carmen didn't look one bit nervous, and it was apparent that she was adoring the attention.

Jo, a brunette with a big personality, had been running her show for seven years. 'What did you do to your arm?' she asked.

'I had an accident,' Carmen explained in clipped English. 'A driver pulled out on a roundabout,' she lied, being the one who had done precisely that. 'Unfortunately, it affected the shoulder I injured as a teenager when a car mowed me down.'

Azize's ears pricked up. Not another one! she thought, feeling resentment for Carmen reminding her of the secret that she tried to keep buried.

'That was pretty unlucky. Did they catch the driver?'

'No, they left me there on the road.' There were gasps from the audience. Saul slurped his beer. 'Great tactic, get the audience's sympathy,' he said.

Azize felt a chill run down her spine.

'What happened?' Jo asked dramatically.
'I had been in England for six months and was staying with a friend. It was a Friday night, and we were at the local pub listening to a popular band at the time. I think they were called something crazy, like Mad Cats.'
'The Mad Dogs, you stupid cow!' Saul shouted at the screen.
Azize brought her hands to her mouth in shock.
'I didn't see what all the fuss was about. I thought the band was boring, so I left and started to walk home. The lane was narrow and poorly lit, and there was a nasty bend. The next thing I knew, I heard screeching tyres, and everything went blank. The driver drove off, and I remember waking up in the hospital. I was lucky to get away with minor injuries, except for my shoulder, of course.'
Saul laughed. Carmen was such a narcissist that she could talk about herself for hours. 'Carry on like this, Jo; then you'll run out of time to ask her about the rest of the crap.'
The sound from the TV faded into the background at Azize's realisation. 'It was her!' she cried. 'I didn't kill anyone! The person I hit is alive—and of all people, it is Carmen Sanchez!' As she processed the information, it felt like an awakening, with all her senses propelled into a new space where nothing else mattered, where all faded into obscurity. For countless years, she had punished herself with panic attacks, nightmares, and feelings of hate and shame towards herself, when all along, the person she thought she had killed survived, and ironically, that person was none other than Carmen Sanchez, or, as Emma had tritely put it, her nemesis.
Like a prisoner casting off her chains and tasting fresh air for the first time in years, Azize found herself in a state of joy she had

never before experienced. She turned off the television and danced around the room.

***

When the dreaded subject came up, Saul held his head in his hands as Carmen began her tirade about how he had pursued her, all lies, of course, as it had been the other way around. He thought about Azize, wondering if she would believe him over Carmen. Then, his phone rang, and it was her. He didn't want to answer, knowing it was the end of everything. All the good times: every memory tarnished like photographs of the past before digital, ripped up and gone forever.

He answered guardedly. 'I told you not to believe her lies.'
'Come over!' Azize said.
'What?'
'Yes, come over!'
'Okay. I'll be there in half an hour.'

Chapter 39

Carmen switched off the TV, satisfied she had come across well. It had been a long day, but it was well worth it. She was enjoying her moment of fame. By portraying herself as the victim and putting her side across, she believed she had successfully restored her reputation. Additionally, she had put Lucia firmly in her place while staving off other potential contenders. But, more than anything, it had been about Saul, and she had accomplished her mission. This evening, karma paid him another visit for his treatment of her. It wasn't just his job he had lost; after tonight, he would say goodbye to his marriage. She smiled. Her work was done.

***

Azize answered the door. 'I checked into number 6 downstairs,' Saul said as he came in. He was tentative and on guard, anticipating an interrogation. Azize walked to the fridge to fetch him a beer. 'Sit down,' she said.
But he remained standing. 'Look!' he said, 'I told you Carmen would lie. It comes down to this: you believe her or me.'
Azize looked him in the eye. 'I didn't watch it all— and I don't care.'

Saul was confused. 'What do you mean? You should at least give me a chance to explain myself.'

'I know what you did; it was deceitful, disloyal, and unforgivable.'

Saul held the unopened bottle between his hands, comforting himself. 'Yes, I know. What can I say when sorry is not enough?'

'I learned a lot tonight, and it's not what you think.' She paused for a moment. 'I learned that secrets eat away at the beholder, hurting them far more than the ones they keep them from.'

Saul nodded, wondering where this was going. 'Yes, I have to agree with you there.'

'But we all have secrets, Saul, and I have harboured one so dark, sinful and evil that it has consumed me with guilt for decades.'

Saul sat down, confused, wondering what on earth was coming next. Was she about to tell him that she had had an affair lasting for years but, unlike his casual liaisons, she had fallen in love with the guy? Andrew perhaps? Was that why he was separating from his wife? He grew nervously impatient as Azize seemed intent on dragging her feet. 'What are you getting at? Spit it out!' he said.

Azize took a deep breath, bracing herself for the revelation that she never thought she would share with anybody. 'Did you hear Carmen talk about a hit-and-run accident?'

'Yes.'

Azize hesitated, but already halfway there, there was no going back. 'It was me!' she declared tearfully. It was out. Using every bit of strength and courage, she'd spoken the words she never thought she would. 'I did it! I didn't mean to, it was an accident, and I panicked,' she went on, but Saul, feeling more relieved than anything, didn't react in the way she expected. Stupidly, he smiled. Azize stared at him in disbelief. 'Why are you smiling? Don't you believe me?'

'No, it's not that. I thought you were about to say you were in love with someone else.'

Azize gasped. 'So, it doesn't matter that I ran someone over? I could have killed her. I drove off, Saul!'

Saul wizened up. 'Okay, I get you.' He looked serious for a moment, then laughed. 'It's in poor taste, but had you finished the job, none of this would have happened,' he said.

At first, Azize was incredulous, but when she saw the irony and felt such relief for having brought her secret to light, she found herself laughing along with him. Then guilt struck her. 'But, Saul, this was serious. It was so wrong of me.'

Saul came to his senses. 'Yes, why did you?'

Azize threw up her hands. 'It was a split decision. I panicked. I couldn't face what I'd done. Part of me thought that if I drove away, I could pretend it never happened. I've never told anyone about this, instead turning the blame in on myself. Soon afterwards, my agoraphobia started. I fooled the therapists my issues were due to abandonment issues, which of course, have had an impact, but I always used it as an excuse. I lied to you, therapists, friends, everyone, even myself. But now that the truth is out, I am relieved of a huge burden.' She looked Saul in the eye. 'Saul, believing you murdered someone, then discovering you didn't is monumental. To me, right now, nothing else matters.'

'Nothing? Not even my inappropriate behaviour?'

Azize smiled at his description of the affair. 'Perhaps that was my karma,' she said. 'Carmen has the right name! I wronged her, and she got me back! I'm not condoning what you did, Saul, because it was wrong. However, think about it another way: had you never slept with her a second time, I would never have found out she survived. I would have gone to my grave ridden with misplaced guilt.'

Saul nodded. Inwardly he was jubilant at the sudden turn of events but tried not to show it. 'Um, things aren't always what they seem, are they?'

Azize threw up her hands. 'Sod karma! Sod Carmen! Sod Orion! Sod work! Sod the media! Sod affairs! Sod everything!' She laughed like a carefree child while Saul looked on in blissful bewilderment at how things had transpired. 'Yes, sod everything!' he smiled, raising his bottle yet to be opened. 'I'll drink to that if you find me a bloody bottle opener!' he laughed.

Azize leapt up to get herself a beer and the bottle opener. 'I have a suggestion,' she said, raising her bottle.

'Okay,' Saul replied.

'Let's put everything behind us!'

Saul smiled. 'I will certainly drink to that!' he said, then gulped down his beer like a man freed from spending a long penance in the desert.

Chapter 40

Five months later

Saul watched Azize playing peek-a-boo with Noah. After the fateful night of Carmen's interview, he had never known her to be as relaxed, and yet things could have been so different had it not been for the strange quirk of fate that liberated her. That was when Saul had vowed never again to take Azize or his marriage for granted. In another universe, he would have got his just desserts, but life had given him another chance, and he wasn't going to blow it this time.

Phoebe, Finn, and Azize laughed as Noah blew raspberries, then chuckled. Family is everything, thought Saul. He had been lucky in more ways than one because Orion's rival, Britannia, had head-hunted him, offering him a job, and he was due to start right after the holiday. It was a desk job, which he was glad about as he had grown weary of chasing his tail travelling around the world, and it meant he would be spending more time at home.

He had no idea why Lady Fortune was smiling down on him but concluded that Emma was right when she said mistakes were opportunities from which to learn and grow, the success of which has the power to nullify the mistake's existence. Never again would he allow his eyes to stray; never again would he behave like the smug, egotistical prat that he used to be. He thought about Carmen, wondering if she had learned from her mistakes. Knowing

Azize's last word

On the night of my revelation, Saul and I closed the door on the past. We never speak of it because it no longer holds relevance for where we stand now. I never found out the entire truth because I chose not to ask. If I had, it would have played on my insecurities, and I doubt we would be together now. Paradoxically, the exposure of our secrets not only served to liberate us but also shaped our future, and consequently, our marriage is stronger than ever.

I decided to cut ties with my parents because there was nothing positive about our relationship, and it served no purpose other than to make me miserable. I wrote them a letter pouring out my feelings and never heard back, endorsing my reason for doing it in the first place. As harsh as it might sound to a bystander, if you walked in my shoes, you would understand why this action has set me free. I have learned to live my truth.

My agoraphobia is improving steadily, even though there are occasions when I suffer a minor blip. But after my breakthrough, I'm aware that the triggers are chiefly from subconscious memory and habit impulses, so I find it easier to deal with.

The last I heard about Carmen was that she returned to Spain. I don't expect to hear from her again because she no longer has power over Saul. She is a troubled woman, and I mean her no harm as long as I never get to see her again!

Do I have any regrets? Aside from the fact I should have stopped the car on that fateful night, none, because I have learned some valuable lessons. I have come to realise that the line between shadow and light is blurry, and sometimes we have to go through the darkness to discover the dawn. As tough as it's been, Saul and I are both wiser and better people for our experiences.

The truth is tricky because it can set you free or devour you. For us, it could so easily have been the latter, but our choices shaped our destiny with blessings. How lucky we are!

> "In all chaos there is a cosmos.
> In all disorder, a secret order."
>
> John Karl Jung

"Tell me the truth of you.
I want to know it all,
All the messed up muddled truth,
And I will tell you mine.
And we can be the secret keepers
Of each other's madness."

Atticus

Author's Page

Originally from southern England, Jane and her husband, Ian, now live in Turkey. The sea and mountains around her provide her with the perfect inspiration for her lifelong love of writing.
These are her other books:

- Allure of the Stone, 2024
- Blessed Be, 2024
- Seeing beyond the Ocean, 2024
- Dream Awake, 2023
- Who Am I? 2022
- Power of the Shadow, 2022
- Dark Star, 2021
- Mirror of Faith, 2019
- Journey to Forever, 2017

"My altars are the mountains and the ocean"
Lord Byron

Milton Keynes UK
Ingram Content Group UK Ltd.
UKHW021054031224
452078UK00010B/630